Virtually Challenged

"An Escort's Story"

Trilogy

J. Asmara

ISBN: 0692794956
ISBN-13: 978-0692794951

This novel is a work of fiction. Any resemblances to actual events, real people, living or dead, organizations, establishments or locales are products of the author's imagination. Other names, characters, places, and incidents are used fictitiously.

Cover Designer: Navi Robins

Because of the dynamic nature of the Internet, any Web addresses or links contained in this book may have changed since publication, and may no longer be valid. The views expressed in this work are solely those of the author and do not necessarily reflect the views of the publisher and the publisher hereby disclaims any responsibility for them.

The material in this book is for mature audiences only and contains graphic sexual content and is intended for those over the age of 18 only. All participants in sexual activities within this book are over the age of 18.

Virtually
CHALLENGED
AN ESCORT'S STORY
J. ASMARA

Prologue

Virtue tipped toed to the bathroom light switch and clicked it off. She did not want her heels to make a sound on the ceramic tiles. Then she climbed into the tub and carefully closed the shower curtain. She listened to the commotion coming from inside of the hotel suite.

"Tony is tired of you dodging him Al. You didn't even tell him you were coming into town. He got to hear it in the streets. Here you go around here renting bitches, going on trips, and wearing tailor suits and shit. Rumor has it that you're even in the pimp business now. Where's Tony's fucking money?" Virtue heard a gentleman say followed by the sound of a fist hitting flesh. She'd laid out flat, attempting to make her body as small as possible.

"Fuck this shit! Vince I don't have no patience for this muthafucka. He ain't about to come up off Tony's money. Let me do this fool," came from an extremely angry guy in between the sound of a cocking gun.

"Calm the fuck down, Bobby. The boss gave me instructions on how to handle this matter. Timing is everything little brother, but you can be the one to do him in when the time comes."

Lord please don't let anyone come in here. Especially not trigger happy Bobby, Virtue thought.

Virtue had been through a lot in her thirty years of life, but nothing as scary as that. She was not even supposed to be there that night. Her loyalty to her childhood friend Sade was how she ended up there with Al. She would have given anything to be at home curled up with Philip instead of lying in a cold tub.

That morning Sade went to Virtue's house and begged her to accompany Albert Castello to a dinner party.

"Sade, I'm out the business. I'm done with that lifestyle," she'd said.

"Your accountant salary cannot allow you to do the things we do and have done; the money, clothes, shoes, and trips. How many people we know can say they've been chartered to private islands?"

"It's more to life than those things. It was fun, but now I want love."

Sade rolled her eyes and said, "Damn, Philip must be laying some good pipe. But I get it. You've always been on that love type shit."

"Glad you understand."

"Please do this very last job for me though. Al is one of my regular sugar daddies. I need to keep him happy. If I could I would, but I have to go handle something for my mom. I need you. Plus you still owe me from that Alfred shit. Please."

Reluctantly Virtue said, "Okay Shay, but this is absolutely it. I mean it."

Virtue laid in the tub thinking of the shoulda-woulda-couldas of the situation. She recalled the many times her Aunt Julia had said, "Always carry yourself as a woman of virtue; virtuous woman that is you. Don't you ever forget that honey."

Not much virtue in parading around town with a different man every night or lying in a tub hoping not to die. You definitely have to make better decisions if you get out of this, she thought.

Suddenly, the circumstances that got her there no longer seemed that serious anymore. Though the three heartbreaks of her life were significant they were not worth losing her life over.

Chapter 1

Taylor Virtue Jones was born in Manhattan, New York at the Bayview Correctional Facility, by way of a crazy situation. Her mother, Stacey Jones had been sentenced to a five year sentence for accessory to murder and aiding and abetting.

One night Taylor's mother drove her father Laurence (a not so law abiding citizen type of guy) to score a hit with his supplier. Three month pregnant Stacey sat and patiently waited outside of the brownstone behind the wheel of their Cadillac Deville.

The two of them made that run together many times prior. However, Stacey did not know that Laurence's plans that particular night was different. He'd gotten tired of being the corner hustle man and wanted a promotion.

Stacey had no worries; she was young, dumb, and in love. She was grooving to Michael Jackson's "Don't Stop 'Til You Get Enough" when she heard a series of gunshots come from inside of the building. Stacey was startled when Laurence snatched the passenger side door open.

"Drive Stacey," he exclaimed as he jumped in the car.

Stacey froze for a second before she responded with, "What? What the hell Laurence?"

"Drive the fucking car and I'll tell you later."

Stacey put the car in drive as two guys came running out of the brownstone and opened fire on their car.

"Oh shit," Stacey said as she floored the gas pedal. "What the fuck Laurence!"

"Just drive."

They rode in silence to the apartment they shared on the other side of the city. Stacey turned the car off and looked at him, "Now do you want to tell me what the hell is going on?" Chyna asked frantically.

"I fucked up. That's what's going on. I told Bruce that it was time for me to have my own block. He pulled his piece out on me. You know I don't do well with threats so I pulled out and shot that motherfucker and one of his boys."

He looked her in her eyes and watched as she processed what he had said.

"We have to get out here. We are going to go up and pack a bag and be out this piece. Stop looking all scared and shit. You know I got you, so let's go," Laurence said.

Reluctantly Stacey got out of the car and followed Laurence to the third floor apartment. She noticed that Laurence had a duffle bag that he had not gone into Bruce's with. There were holes in Laurence's story but with the history of violence in their relationship, Stacey was not going to question him.

Stacey and Laurence packed and went across the bridge to New Jersey. They hid out there for two weeks before they were caught. Laurence ended up at Sing Sing and Stacey at Bayview. Stacey got five years and Laurence was sentenced to forty years.

The story that Laurence had told Stacey was far from the truth. What actually transpired that night was that Laurence went to the apartment with the intent to take over Bruce's empire by force and not by promotion. Laurence like many of Bruce's dealers was blinded by the green eyed monster.

When Laurence went to Bruce's that night his intent was to rob him of all his drugs and leave him with a bullet in his head. He chose that night because Bruce was supposed to be alone. He'd ordered the gang to go on a run upstate. What Laurence did not know was at the last minute Bruce had instructed his next in command "Slick" and two of his goons, "Black" and "Blue" to stay behind.

When Laurence arrived, Blue greeted him at the door where they dapped each other up. Blue escorted Laurence to Bruce's office where he was seated behind the desk. Bruce got up from behind the large oak desk to greet him when Laurence pulled out his gun and shoot Bruce in his chest. He shot Blue in his head before he had time to grab for his gun.

Laurence grabbed a bag filled with dope that sat beside the desk. Then he grabbed Bruce's money clip out of his pocket and left out of the room. He'd made it down the hall when Slick and Black came running from the upstairs and started shooting at him.

Laurence escaped with a minor wound from a bullet that grazed his arm. He made it out of the brownstone and to Stacey who sat in the getaway car.

The events of that night completely changed the blueprint of Taylor's life. The day Taylor was born her mother's brother Bryant and his wife Julia drove to New York from South Carolina and picked her up. The predestined city girl was raised in Beaufort, South Carolina on Saint Helena Island. Instead of roaming the streets of Brooklyn, she ran up and down dirt roads barefooted.

Taylor grew up in the church; Bryant was a Deacon and Julia a Deaconess. Despite the circumstances in which Taylor entered the world Julia always believed she was destined for greatness; hence her giving her the name Virtue.

Taylor had a normal childhood. She was the only child in the home because Julia and Bryant were unable to conceive. Her aunt and uncle insured that all of her needs were met and she was protected from the influences of the world.

Things started to change for Taylor once she got into high school. She started to find fault in her sheltered but safe life. She wanted to be like the other children who were going to parties and dating.

During her freshman year, Taylor became rebellious. She began skipping school; she almost spent more time away from school than in attendance. The honor roll became a faded memory in her and her aunt and uncle's minds.

Nothing that Bryant or Julia said or did was right in Taylor's eyes. She felt like she had all of the answers, though they'd lived many more years than she had. That especially became apparent when her five feet even body began to develop.

Though pint size, Taylor had the confidence and toughness of someone that was six feet tall. Her milk chocolate skin was flawless and she had features that could be seen in any catalog. It didn't take her long to learn how to work her full C cup breast, small waist, and fat ass to her advantage.

Taylor's partners in crime were her best friends Chyna Mack and Sade Walker. If you saw one the others weren't far behind; teachers called them the three musketeers. The girl's common ground were absentee fathers. They all longed for that male figure in their lives. Though Taylor had Bryant in the picture, he was hardly around due to his multiple side businesses.

Chyna's parents were divorced and she hardly seen her father. Chyna was the more responsible one of the group. Taylor called her the nerdy cheerleader. She was a varsity cheerleader as a freshman and maintained a three point five grade point average. Cheerleading was her life. At five feet nine inches she towered over the other girls and commanded attention. Chyna was a natural beauty with her black and Dominican background. Her bronzed skin always looked like she just stepped off the beach. She always wore her jet black wavy hair down framing her almond shaped face.

Sade had a different story. She was the product of rape and never knew her father. She allowed that to take over her life. Sade was reckless; she hardly thought logically or responsibly. The fact that she had already gotten her grown up body at only fourteen did not help either. Sade fancied dating men between the ages of twenty one and twenty nine. The men never thought twice looking at the young lady that always wore clothes that showcased her big titties and ass. Lil Kim was her idol and she mirrored her style after her.

Taylor, Chyna, and Sade searched in not so good places for that male attention they lacked. They were drawn to the bad boys; the popular for the wrong reason boys. Against Bryant and Julia's guidance, Taylor began dating a young man named Victor.

Victor was the type of person who pushed boundaries. He was what the old people called "no mannered". Victor did what he wanted, when he wanted to with no regards to authority or consequence. Taylor being the child with nothing but rules, envied Victor. The envy progressed into a relationship during one of her many trips to in school suspension.

Taylor and Victor had been dating for about three months when he approached her with the proposition to skip school for the first time.

"You wanna skip fourth period with me?" he asked as they walked down the hall.

"I don't know. I'm scared."

"What are you scared for?"

"You know I can't get caught. My uncle would have a fit."

"Well, we aren't gonna get caught."

"How do you know that?"

"Cause I do it all the time. All you have to do is move to the gym after we get out of third period. Once you get there, go around the gym instead of inside. Make sure you go around the right side so nobody sees you. My cousin will be there to pick us up. Look for a white Honda Accord. His name is Justin if I'm not there by the time you get there."

Nervously Taylor said, "Okay."

She knew she should have said no, but it was something about Victor that always compelled her to do whatever he wanted her to.

Taylor could not concentrate throughout the entire third period. She was so nervous about her school skipping experience. She replayed Victor's instructions several times in her head. When Taylor looked at the clock on the wall, she saw that there was only five minutes left in her English class. She could hear every second tick away on the clock.

Finally the bell rang. Taylor grabbed her bag and went out into the hall. She'd begun her stroll toward the gym when somebody grabbed her arm. Taylor was afraid to turn around because she thought she was caught. Her heart beat was the only sound that Taylor heard as she stood there frozen.

"Tay what the hell is wrong with you? You didn't hear me talking to you?" Taylor turned and focused on an angry looking Sade.

"Are you high or something?" Sade continued.

Taylor took a deep breath and responded with, "Shay I'm glad it's you."

"What's your deal? I'd been calling your name ever since you walked out of Mrs. Johnson's class."

"My bad girl. I've been zoned. Victor wants me to skip next period with him."

"Are you going?"

"Yeah, but I'm scared."

"Don't be. Just be careful. I'll cover for you."

"Thanks Hun."

"No problem, don't do nothing I wouldn't."

"Hell, what wouldn't you do?"

The girls laughed as Taylor continued on her journey.

The late bell rang just as she began on the right side of the gym. Once Taylor got around the gym, she saw the Honda parked by the side walk. She picked up her pace when she saw Victor sitting in the front seat. He smiled and then turned to say something to the guy in the driver's seat. Taylor was a bottle of nerves by the time she reached the car.

"Taylor this is Justin, Justin this is Taylor," Victor said as she got into the backseat.

"Hey," Taylor said timidly.

She still expected the principal or some other faculty member to come out and catch her in her skipping attempt. That panic was short lived as Justin pulled out of the parking spot. Taylor sat quietly as the guys talked in the front seat.

Man I hope no one who knows Aunt Julia or Uncle Bryant see me, she thought as she watched from the backseat.

Justin drove through Beaufort. They ended their journey at a house on Pigeon Pointe Road. Taylor hesitated to get out of the car.

"Come on Taylor," Victor said as he opened her door.

He's such a gentleman, Taylor thought. Or was he? Taylor left her innocence in that house that day and would later find out she was sleeping with the enemy.

Taylor was head over heels in love with Victor. She felt that everything she and Victor did together was special; to include their weekly skipping sessions. Taylor was quite content in her teenage love affair. However, all of that changed one afternoon when Taylor learned of Victor's devious motives. He invited Justin to partake in Taylor's prize.

"What are you doing?" Taylor asked as she attempted to cover her naked body.

"Be easy babes. It's only my cousin. If you love me like you say you do, then you'd do it for me."

"But-"

"Ain't no but. Do it for me."

"Okay," Taylor said half-heartedly.

It slowly became obvious to Taylor that Victor did not care for her as he claimed. The sharing Taylor with Justin turned into him sharing her with his friends; whom he got paid by.

Taylor naively put up with Victor and his demoralizing treatment. It was not until she said no to Victor's friend Derrick that she had enough. Taylor told Derrick that she was not going to have sex with him, and he took it. Victor did not come to her rescue as she screamed and fought Derrick.

During the act Taylor thought of the mother that she ridiculed; the mother who's footsteps she was following. Once Stacey got out of prison she took to the New York streets. She got turned out on crack and started hooking to get her fix. Stacey hooked for years with no regards to the child she had in South Carolina. Taylor was thirteen years old when her mom died from acquired immune deficiency syndrome.

When her mother died Taylor made a vow to never let any man dictate her life.

As Taylor stood there pinned in a corner being violated from the back, she refused to be used any more. Taylor never told anyone about the incident because she felt no one would believe a “hoe”. She broke up with Victor and never looked his way again. Taylor turned cold and desensitized by sex. From that day on, sex became a means to getting what she wanted; which was usually a nut.

Chapter 2

The brokenness Taylor felt from Victor's betrayal motivated her to be better; to show him that he was a fool. Taylor made it through high school. Though she skipped regularly she managed to maintain a three point one grade point average.

Taylor, Chyna, and Sade all left Beaufort and moved to Columbia. Living in the capital city was a longtime dream of the girls. Taylor and Chyna attended the University of South Carolina. Sade on the other hand had no desire to go to college. However, she always had a knack for doing hair so she enrolled in Kenneth Shuler School of Cosmetology.

Life for the girls was good. They shared a three bedroom apartment near the USC campus. Taylor enjoyed the freedom that she had being away from Beaufort; free from the rules that Bryant and Julia had in place. There wasn't anyone telling her what to do and/or how to do it. Anytime she had a chance to, she let her wild side out.

Taylor's promiscuous behavior continued when she went to college. She quickly got bored with college boys and during her sophomore year she moved to the "ballers". She'd gone through several street corner hustlers that year.

It was Taylor's junior year when she met William Braxton James and things changed. With a name like that one would assume he was an upstanding citizen. Contrary to the desires of his mother, William also known as Bam, was anything but.

The night she and William met Taylor, Chyna, and Sade had went out to celebrate the ending of midterms. They decided to go to a club called Esquire.

"I hope this place ain't lame," Sade said on their way.

"Me either," Chyna cosigned.

"Y'all need to stop cause you know we make the party," Taylor said with a smile. "But I've heard it be jumping out there."

"I hope so cause I'm looking good as a motherfucker tonight. I hope there's some ballers out there cause I'm in need of a shopping trip," Sade said.

Taylor never knew how Sade pulled it off but guys always spent crazy amounts of money on her. Sade made the gifts Taylor got look like nothing. Taylor was more turned on by the control and mind set of the bad boys versus the benefits. The only benefit she was concerned about was a big, hard dick.

When Taylor pulled up to Esquire the parking lot was full.

"Hell yeah," Sade exclaimed as she adjusted her boobs in her push up bra. "Mama needs some new shoes."

Taylor and Chyna laughed at her but they knew she was very serious. While they had to work part time jobs as well as did work study at school to make it, Sade's part of the rent was usually gifted. Sade was about her money. Her motto was, "If it don't make money it don't make sense." Taylor didn't know if it was her big ass or nice tits that men gravitated to, but they did.

The ladies walked in Esquire like they owned the place. They headed straight to the dance floor because they loved to dance. They danced a few songs and then found a seat near the club's VIP section.

"Damn, y'all look at all that eye candy over in the VIP section," Sade said.

"You always looking for some dick Sade. We're just here to have a good time," Chyna chimed in.

"Whatever bitch, you need some dick in your life."

"Whatever."

"Play nice ladies," Taylor said in between her laughter.

****

William sat high in the VIP section of Esquire overlooking the club. He was happy because the club was packed that night. Through the crowd he saw Taylor lead Chyna and Sade to the dance floor.

William watched as Taylor rolled her hips on the dance floor. He was mesmerized by the way she moved. *Damn, she sexy than a motherfucker. I ain't never seen her before.*

"Bam do you hear me? Over there zoned out and shit."

"Oh shit, my bad," he said to his right hand man Benny.

William and Benny had been friends since they were in the second grade. They did some of the grimiest shit together. The type of things that once it's done, it's never spoken of again. William had not gotten his nickname Bam because of his gushing good looks but because of his ability to knock a motherfucker out with no remorse. Not only had he knocked out his share of guys, he was also known to carry a gun. The name Bam carried a lot of weight on the streets.

"What are you over there thinking about?"

"Look at shorty right there in the purple dress."

"She's nice."

"Yeah, I've never seen shorty in here before. Have you?"

"Nah."

"I definitely need to holla at her. For sure," William said biting his bottom lip.

William watched Taylor as she, Chyna, and Sade got a table.

"A Benny tell Mecco to come here please bro."

"Aight."

Mecco was one of his workers; he was who you'd classify as William's goon. Some people called him William's "bitch boy." Mecco didn't care though, because being on William's payroll was compensation enough for the hate. Plus, no one had the balls to say it to Mecco's face; the face that was on the head of a six foot five, two hundred seven pounds of muscled beast.

"What up boss?" Mecco said as he came to William.

"I need you to do me a favor. You see that honey right there?" he said pointing at Taylor.

"The one in the purple or red?"

"Purple."

"Yeah."

"I want you to invite her, and her friends I guess, to join me. Be sure to handle it in a sensitive less aggressive manner."

"Got ya boss."

William watched as Mecco went to their table. They exchanged words for a few minutes and Mecco walked back... alone.

****

Taylor, Sade, and Chyna were laughing and having a good time when Mecco approached Taylor at the table.

"Hello ladies."

"Hello," they said.

"Miss, my man Bam wants you and your friends to join him in the VIP section."

"I don't know your man. Plus I don't jump because someone says to."

Sade kicked Taylor under the table and gave her the "what the hell" look.

"Tell your man that unless his legs are broke he can step to me himself."

Mecco stood there for a minute in shock.

"Do you not know who Bam is?"

"I don't give a damn if he's the President of the United States. I'm still not going to jump for him."

"Well alright then," he said as he walked off back to the club's VIP section to relay Taylor's message.

"What was up with that Tay? We could be in VIP right now," Sade said. "You know the ballers be in VIP."

"Girl please. You know I don't run behind no man. They step to me."

"That's why your ass keep hooking up with them wanna-bes."

"Whatever Shay."

"You know I'm telling the truth."

"Y'all stop. I'm not drunk enough to put up with y'all and y'all baller bullshit. I'm going to get a drink," Chyna said as she got up and went to the bar.

Sade got up from the table as well, "I'm about to get a drink too. Want a Coke or something?"

"Nah I'm good."

Sade and Chyna loved going out with Taylor because she didn't drink; she was always a dependable designated driver.

"Alright. I'll be back."

Taylor was dancing in her seat and watching the dance floor when William tapped her on her shoulder. Taylor had to do a double take when she turned around. William was a good looking man; tall, built, nice smile, and big feet. Everything about him screamed sexy as hell to Taylor.

"Hello beautiful. I was told that I had to come over here and holla at you because you declined my invitation."

Taylor had gotten wrapped up in the way his mouth formed his words and could not respond.

"So do you mind if I sit down with you?"

Taylor shook her head no.

"Well I'm Will, my boys call me Bam though. What's your

name?"

Taylor had to take a hard swallow before she spoke because all she could think about was if his male member was as lovely as what she could see before her.

"I'm Taylor. My girls call me Tay."

"Nice to meet you Taylor. I like your style. I've been watching you since you walked in. Would you do me the honor of being my guest in the VIP section?"

The smile he shot her at the end would make any woman accompany him anywhere and do anything when she got there.

"Okay, but my girls are at the bar."

"That's cool. We can talk until they come back."

He scooted his chair closer to Taylor.

"I want to make sure I don't miss anything," he said flashing that winning smile. "I've never seen you here before. Do you live here in Columbia or you just visiting?"

"I live here. I go to USC."

"Beauty and brains. I like it."

Taylor couldn't help but blush.

"Me and my girls are here celebrating the end of midterms. I heard about this place so we came to check it out."

"So what do you think so far?"

"It's a real cool atmosphere. I like it."

"Well thank you."

"You must work here."

"Actually, I own it."

"Wow," she said as Chyna and Sade returned.

"Hello ladies. I'm Will."

"I'm Shay."

"And I'm Chyna."

"Nice to meet you. Your beautiful friend has accepted my invitation for you lovely ladies to accompany me and my friends in the VIP section."

Sade was smiling from ear to ear. Taylor knew she saw dollar signs behind the invitation.

William got up and pulled Taylor's chair from the table and grabbed her hand, "Follow me ladies."

Taylor was impressed with the fact that Will was such a gentleman. He was different from the other guys she'd dealt with. That along with some other perks is what eventually kept Taylor around.

They entered the area and Will introduced them to his entourage. Sade immediately set her eyes on a guy named Tim. Tim looked like he was straight out of a rap video; gold teeth, cornrows, fly outfit, and Jordan's. She was on him like white on rice.

Chyna sat and sipped her Sex on the Beach while she plotted on the drinks they had displayed on a nearby table. She planned to get wasted; especially with free liquor.

Will focused all of his attention on Taylor. He made her feel like she was the only woman in the club. The DJ called for the last dance and Will grabbed Taylor to dance; Usher's "Slow Jam" was playing. They danced and then he walked the ladies to Taylor's car.

"You drive safe. I'm going to close up here and call you if that's okay."

"Okay."

"Talk to you soon."

Sade couldn't wait for them to pull off, "So..."

"I think I've hit the jackpot. He's fine, a gentleman, and owns his own club."

"What? He owns Esquire?"

"Yep."

Sade let out a squeal, "Bitch you about to come up."

"Girl stop. We just met."

"Fuck all that. He's feeling the shit out of you. Better seal that shit before somebody else do."

"Shay shut the fuck up with all that noise," Chyna said.

"Chyna shut your drunk ass up and ride," Sade spat back at Chyna.

"Don't tell me to shut up and I'm not drunk. Thank you very much," Chyna slurred.

Though Chyna was the quieter, more mild mannered one of the group liquor brought out a louder more outspoken Chyna. Taylor and Sade never paid her any attention when she was on her drunken tangents. They continued their gitty school girl conversation on their new prospects while Chyna went to sleep.

"I'm hooking up with Tim tomorrow. Maybe we should all hang out," Sade began to plot.

"Damn Shay, I don't even know if he's going to call and you already making plans."

"You know he's gonna call. They always call; you too fine for him not to."

"True. When we talk I'll mention it to him."

They made it home. Taylor and Sade helped Chyna up the steps to their apartment. They got her into the apartment and into her bedroom. After getting Chyna into bed Taylor went and showered. She'd just gotten out the shower when her cell phone rang. She smiled when she saw it was Will.

"Hello."

"Hey lil mama. You made it home?"

"Yeah. I just got out of the shower."

"I bet that's a nice sight."

"Yes, it is."

"Hmmmm. Look, I want to see you. You up for some early morning breakfast?"

"When?"

"Right now. How about we meet at that Waffle House by the university?"

"Alright. Give me a few to throw some clothes on. I'll be there in thirty minutes."

"I'll be there waiting."

"Okay."

They hung up and Taylor got dressed. She threw on a fitted top, sweats, and Nike's; total opposite of the fitted dress and high heels she'd had on at the club. She wasn't tripping because she knew her body would be banging in a potato sack.

Taylor pulled up to the Waffle House and immediately knew which car was Will's. There was an all black BMW with limo tint and chrome rims in the parking lot that put Taylor's Honda Civic to shame.

Will went to her car and greeted her with a hug, "Glad you came."

Taylor knew the hug was to feel her up, but she didn't mind at all.

"Damn you look good in them sweats."

"Stop it," she said playfully.

"Nah, for real. I love a woman who looks good in regular real shit. Anybody can look good half naked in club clothes with a ton of makeup. But it's something special to have that natural beauty; which you have so you got my vote."

"Well I'm glad to hear that," Taylor said as they walked into the Waffle House.

Will and Taylor spent nearly three hours at the restaurant talking. By the time they'd left, Taylor was in deep like with Will. She welcomed the idea of letting Will into her world, but she never expected the joy and pain that would come from that decision.

Chapter 3

Taylor and Will had been dating for months and things were going pretty well for her. Will showered her with gifts galore; clothes, shoes, designer handbags, and jewelry. There was nothing he wouldn't have done for Taylor. She had fallen for Will hard.

It was Will and Taylor's six month anniversary. Will called Taylor to tell her he had a special evening with a big surprise for her. She loved surprises and was super excited to see what Will had in store.

Taylor had begun her preparation for the evening. Sade did her hair and then she went to the mall to get an outfit. Taylor had just walked out of New York And Company when she was approached by a pregnant young lady.

"Excuse me. Are you Taylor?" she asked.

"Yes," Taylor said slowly. "Do I know you?"

"No, but you know my old man."

"And who is your old man?"

"Bam."

"Oh really?"

"Yes and this is his baby. So I would appreciate it if you leave him alone because he will never leave me alone. We have too much history boo."

Taylor's pulse quickened as she stood there. She didn't hear anything else the lady said because she was in a daze. *Ain't no fucking way that motherfucker playing me*, she thought as she tried to maintain her cool.

"Okay whatever your name is-"

"It's Jasmine."

"Well thank you Jasmine. You have a good day and I wish you and Will the best," she said as she walked away. *Never let a bitch see you sweat.*

Jasmine's words cut Taylor deep. Will was the first guy she'd let get close to her since her relationship with Victor and her emotions were all over the place.

Taylor called Sade as soon as she got in her car.

"Hey girl. How'd the shopping go? Found anything?"

"Actually I got more than I bargained for at the mall," Taylor said softly.

"What's wrong Tay?"

"So I'm at the mall and this chick comes at me and tells me that she's Will's old lady."

"Damn."

"That's not even the worst part. She's pregnant."

"Holy shit!"

"Right. Like big as shit pregnant."

"That motherfucker."

"Exactly."

"So what you gonna do?"

"What you mean? I'm going to stop fucking with him."

"Just like that?"

"Yes."

"You ain't even gonna call him out on his shit? Tay, don't fuck up your payday on some bitch's word. You know you be all emotional and shit. Fuck that. That motherfucker's paper has been paying your part of the rent and keeping your pockets stacked. Just saying."

"You're right Shay. But that shit still hurts."

"I know but just don't react hastily because of your emotions. Don't be no fool."

"Okay. Thanks girl. I'm about to go by the club and talk to him."

"Okay. Call me if you need me."

Taylor hung up and drove to Esquire.

****

Will, Benny, Tim, and Mecco were in the office at Esquire.

"What the fuck went wrong?" Will exclaimed.

"Jerome's spot got hit," Tim said.

"I'm getting tired of so much incompetent motherfuckers around me. For real," Will said.

"Motherfuckers getting too comfortable and shit. Jerome just brought on some more crew. I wouldn't be surprised if it was an inside job," Tim added.

"So how much of my shit's gone?" Will said in an agitated tone.

"All of it."

"Bruh, that's ten thousand motherfucking dollars," Will said with flaring nostrils.

"Bam. This is the second time some shit has popped off at Jerome's spot. I think we need to handle this and cut that leg off," Tim said.

"Yo Bam, I agree with Tim. We need to handle it with finesse though," Benny interjected.

Will nodded his head agreeing.

"First, Mecco I want you to go pick Jerome's ass up and bring him to see me. The fact that he hadn't contacted me yet is shady in itself, but we're going to play it cool."

"Gotcha boss," Mecco said as he moved to the door.

When he walked out Will turned to Tim and Benny, "Keep y'all ears close to the ground. I feel like some shit's brewing in the streets. You know we got enemies who want to see us fail."

"Cool," Tim said. "I'm about to dip out and holla at Bones. Hit me up on the hip if you hear anything else."

"You bet."

"One."

"One."

Tim gave Will some dap and left out as well.

"Look Bam you know you're my boy, my brother, and I have your back but we need to talk on some real shit."

"What Benny?"

"I think it's time for you to get out the game. We've been doing this shit since high school. Shit's feeling real fucked up in my gut. You opened this club as nothing more than a cover up gig. It's one of the hottest spots in Columbia now and is bringing in a lot of money. You might need to be Bam the club owner and not Bam the drug dealer. You done got rid of Jasmine crazy ass and you all into shorty. I think your punk ass might even be in love," Benny added with a laugh, "You might need to chill for a while."

"Benny you know the streets is my life."

"True, but you can start a new life. Just something to think about bro, but you're my man regardless."

"Thanks man."

There was a knock at the door. "Come in," Will said.

Taylor walked in.

"Hey babe," he said as he got up. "What you doing here?"

"We need to talk," she said matter-a-factly.

Benny got up. "Hey Taylor. Bam I'll get at you later man."

"What's wrong baby? I'm not liking that look on your face or that tone?"

"Who the fuck is Jasmine Will?"

"Some broad I used to fuck with."

"Used to fuck with? Not your old lady? Not your baby mama?"

"Nah. Babe calm down and have a seat."

Taylor sat down and Will sat down by her.

"Jasmine was my jump off for a while."

"Jump off?"

"Yeah. We'd hook up, have sex, I'd throw her a little money

every now and then. That's all."

"What about the baby?"

"I don't even know if that baby's mine. When I told her I wasn't fucking with her no more she came with that baby bullshit."

"Why you hadn't told me any of this before now?"

"Because it wasn't an issue and I was focused on us and getting to know everything I could about you. How did you find out about her anyways?"

"She approached me at the mall. She knew my name and everything."

Will grabbed Taylor and pulled her close to him, "You don't have to worry about none of those chicken heads out there in them streets. I have what I want. Yes I have a past but you are my present and hopefully my future."

Will kissed Taylor and the warmth that went through her body made her forget about her concerns.

"We're still on for tonight right?"

"Yes," Taylor said still engulfed in the lingering kiss.

"Good. I'll pick you up at seven. Pack an overnight bag."

"Okay."

"Now get your fine ass out of here so I can wrap up here. You know I can't focus with you around."

Taylor smiled as she was sent off with a kiss.

Damn, Will thought as he picked up the phone and dialed Jasmine's number.

"What?"

"What you mean what? Don't play with me Jas. I'm not in the mood for your shit today."

"Guess your little girlfriend went running to you. What you doing with that young ass girl when you got all this grown woman over here any fucking way?"

"So what are you trying to prove Jas? Not happy with our arrangement anymore?"

"Fuck that bullshit ass arrangement!"

"No. What's going to happen is you play your role and stay the fuck out of what me and Taylor have going on. Once the baby's born then we'll go from there. So keep your hormonal ass still."

"Whatever. I'm tired of you and these bitches you pick up because you always come back to me."

"Not this time Jas so chill the fuck out."

"We'll see," Jasmine said before she hung up.

Bitch!

****

Taylor left out of Esquire with a little bit of a bounce to her step. She was already excited about the surprise Will had, but now knowing they were also going away somewhere was the icing on the cake.

She had just reached her car when Mecco pulled in front of the club in his Suburban. As she sat there she saw Mecco snatch Jerome out of the truck. *Wonder what that's about?* she thought as her eyes focused in on Jerome. She didn't know him but it was evident that his face lost a fight with someone's fist. *Damn, somebody messed him up.*

Taylor always had an uneasy feeling about Mecco, but that day his facial expression was more creepy than usual.

Taylor was still pondering the situation when Chyna called her.

"Hello."

"Hey Tay. Where are you?"

"About to leave Esquire. Why what's up?"

"My car won't start. Can you pick me up from campus?"

"Yeah. I'm on my way."

"Thanks girl. I'll be in the library. Call me when you get close."

"Okay."

Taylor drove off and didn't give any more thought to the Mecco and Jerome situation.

Once she and Chyna got home, Taylor packed her bag and began her transformation for her evening with Will. She'd bought a red fitted tank dress that she paired with a tailored black blazer and black platform pumps. Taylor was putting on her lipstick when Sade came in her room.

"Damn girl you look good. Poor Will ain't gonna be able to contain himself."

"That's my goal," she stated with a smirk.

"Guess you decided to keep seeing him."

"Yeah. He said him and that girl are over and he doesn't even know if the baby is his. I believe him so that's that."

"Well alright then. Come in my room when you're done with your makeup so I can put some more mousse on your hair. I'm loving that deep wave on you; you're rocking that shit for real."

"Thanks Shay, but you know it's because I have the best hair stylist there is."

Sade smiled and left out of Taylor's room. Taylor heard a knock on the apartment door and shortly after Will came into her room.

"Hey baby. Damn you look good," he said before he laid a sensual kiss on her.

"Thank you baby. Only the best when I'm stepping out with my man."

"You're doing that. You got me wanting to take you right here. You lucky I have something planned for you."

Taylor laughed, "Well then, on that note we should get to this surprise evening."

Will grabbed Taylor's bag and they left out of the apartment.

"So are you going to tell me what you have up your sleeves?"

"No, it's a surprise."

"Awe. Okay, guess I have to wait."

"Yes. I promise that you will enjoy it."

"I'm sure I will," she said with a smile.

Will drove approximately an hour outside of Columbia. By the time they got to their destination (a bed and breakfast) it was dark. Taylor admired the lights that illuminated the yard of the establishment; which was a restored plantation home.

"This is really pretty Will."

"Wait until you see the inside. You're going to love it."

Will was not wrong about that. It was so far from the realm of anything that Taylor had ever experienced throughout her whole life. She was so excited that she could not focus on any one thing. Her eyes bounced from the huge wooden staircase, to the Victorian furniture, to the grand chandeliers as Will spoke to the clerk.

"Yes Mr. James. Here are your keys and the dinner you requested will be served in about ten minutes."

"Thank you."

"You're very welcome. Let me get those bags for you."

Will grabbed Taylor's hand and they followed the clerk to their room. The room was decorated elegantly in sky blue and chocolate with gold accents throughout. The focal point of the room was the bed. Taylor had shared with Will that as a child she'd always dreamt of having a canopy bed. She felt like it showed prestige; it was what she envisioned a queen would sleep in. Not only had Will listened to her but also provided her the opportunity to live out a childhood dream for a night.

"Would you like for me to ring you when the dinner preparations are complete?" Taylor heard the clerk ask as she went looking around in the bathroom.

Gorgeous, she thought when she saw the claw foot tub that was in the middle of the room. She had gotten lost in the elegance of the room and did not realize that Will had come in the bathroom. He hugged her from behind, "Do you like it?" he asked softly in her ear.

"I love it. It's a beautiful place."

"Good. I want this to be the first of many anniversaries we share."

"Sounds good to me."

"Good," he said with a big smile.

"Though I don't know how you're going to top this on our one year anniversary."

"I have an idea," he said as he spun Taylor around and kissed her.

Taylor felt the hardness of his manhood as their bodies were pressed together. Will lifted Taylor up and carried her to the bed. They were heavy in their groping when a buzzer went off on an intercom near the door. *He literally meant he would buzz us,* Taylor thought and chuckled.

"Damn, I almost forget about dinner."

"Fuck dinner."

Will laughed. "You are something else. They prepared something special for us so we can't flake. But trust me when I tell you that you will be my dessert with your fine ass."

The buzzer went off again. Will went to the intercom and pushed the button. "Yes."

"Mr. James your dinner is ready."

"Thank you. We will be down momentarily."

Will went back over to Taylor. He briefly took her breath away when he leaned over her. Taylor was so in love with Will that she could hardly contain herself. She anticipated his every kiss, touch, and embrace.

Will kissed her lightly and said, "Let's go my love."

They went down the stairs and were led to a patio off of a small room at the back of the bed and breakfast. Lights and candles lit up the area. Will pulled out a chair that was at the lone table in the center of the patio. Once Will sat down a gentleman came out with an ice chest with a bottle of champagne.

"Hello my name is Chris and I have the pleasure of serving you this evening."

Chris opened the bottle and gave them each a glass of champagne.

"I will return with an appetizer," Chris said before walking off.

Will handed Taylor her glass and picked his up.

"Baby you know I don't drink."

"It's just champagne Taylor."

"You know I'm a light weight."

"Well, you're safe with me. So I want to make a toast to us and our lasting love."

Taylor smiled as they clanked their glasses. Chris came back with a crab cake appetizer. The remainder of the four course meal consisted of lightly dressed salad, lobster and steak, and molten chocolate cake.

Taylor and Will ate under the stars and engaged in deep conversation. It was during dessert when the champagne hit Taylor. An electric current traced her entire body from the inside and exploded out of her vagina opening. Her body screamed to be touched by Will.

Taylor dipped her finger into chocolate center of the molten cake. She licked the chocolate off seductively while staring into Will's eyes. She let out a soft moan as she sucked her finger.

"I'm ready to go back to the room. How about you?" Taylor said.

"Hell yeah," Will exclaimed.

He thanked the staff for accommodating them before he and Taylor went to their room. Will had just locked the door when Taylor pushed him on the door and kissed him passionately as she stroked his third leg.

Taylor was never timid when it came to love making but she was extra forceful that night. She undid Will's belt and pants and pulled his penis out. Taylor got on her knees and put it in her mouth. Will leaned on the door and braced himself as she gave him some head. Taylor sucked him until he felt like he was about to cum.

"Damn baby, you gonna make me cum. I don't want to yet." Will stood Taylor up and said, "Lay your fine ass on that bed."

Will came out of his clothes and Taylor had taken of her blazer. She started to take off her pumps when Will stopped her.

"No, leave those on," he said as he pulled her dress over her head.

"Nice," he said when he saw the bra and panty set she'd gotten from Victoria's Secret.

Will laid Taylor back on the bed and kissed her up and down her legs before he put her legs on his shoulders. Will massaged her clitoris with his thumb and kissed her pussy hole. Taylor rolled her hips and pulled him in with her thighs.

Will's tongue moved to Taylor's clitoris. He flicked and sucked her clit the way she liked it. Taylor came multiple times in his mouth. Her heartbeat raced and she was eager to feel him within her walls. Will raised Taylor's hips and licked her with an intensified speed. He used just enough pressure that made her volcano erupt. Taylor let out a shrill of pure pleasure as her juices flowed.

Taylor was still wrapped in the exhilarated after math of her orgasm when Will entered her with his manhood. She bit her lip to avoid letting out a loud squawk of enjoyment. He did every variation of the missionary position that he knew to do. Taylor rewarded his dedication with the showering of her juices.

Will flipped Taylor around and entered her from the back.

"I love the way that ass looks when my dick's between them cheeks," Will said as he smacked her on her ass.

Will's thrusts were so intense that Taylor could no longer contain her screams. She buried her screams of pleasure into a pillow as Will gave it to her from the back.

Their bodies became one as Taylor threw her body back in rhythm with Will's. They danced to their own music around the entire bed. The dance of love ended with an "I love you Taylor" from Will before he released his love juice inside of her.

Will was always careful up to that point, but he'd made up in his mind that he wanted Taylor to have his child. The aftershock of her orgasm was so intense that she never gave the fact that he came inside of her any thought. She laid in his embrace and went to sleep.

****

Will woke up before Taylor did and he watched her sleep. *She's so beautiful. We are going to have a beautiful baby. Benny may be on to something, it might be time to get out of the game.*

Taylor woke up.

"Good morning."

"Good morning."

"Were you watching me sleep again?" she asked and smiled.

"Of course," Will said before kissing her on the forehead.

"You're beautiful when you're asleep. Plus that's the only time you're quiet," he added playfully.

"Whatever," Taylor said with a laugh.

"I'm just playing baby. Breakfast is in a little over an hour. How about I run you a bath and then we relax until breakfast?"

"That sounds good, because I'm dying to get in that tub. You gonna join me?"

"I'm not sure if both of us will fit. It looks pretty small."

"I think we can make it work," Taylor said with a sneaky tone.

"Sounds like you're trying to get fresh with me."

"And if I am?" she said with a kiss.

"I'd like it."

They both laughed and Will went to fill the tub. Taylor went into the bathroom behind him. They brushed their teeth while the tub filled.

Will had just finished brushing his teeth when his phone went off. It was a text message from Benny. *"It's done."* Will placed the phone on the nightstand and went back into the bathroom. He walked in just as Taylor dropped the complimentary robe she had been wearing.

"Hmmmmm..." he said as he approached her with a kiss. "I'll never get tired of looking at you."

"Oh yeah? I hope not."

"Yeah. I wasn't playing when I told you I love you. I want you to be my future."

"This is the second time you've said that."

"Yes, because I feel it in my soul," Will paused and pulled a ring box out of the pocket of his robe. Taylor stood with her mouth open as Will got down on one knee. He opened the box and exposed a two carat diamond ring.

"I know it's only been six months but it's been the best six months of my life. Marry me Taylor."

"Wow. This is crazy. Wow. I don't know what to say."

"Say yes."

"Yes," she exclaimed.

Will scooped Taylor up and kissed her passionately. They forgot about both the bath and breakfast. They made love until it was time for them to checkout.

Chapter 4

The weeks following Taylor and Will's anniversary getaway were a little hectic. Not only was the school year coming to an end but Taylor had been receiving grief from her aunt and uncle about her marrying Will. They never approved of her dating him. Her Aunt Julia always referred to him as "that hoodlum". There was no way that she could tell them that she was pregnant. She hadn't even had the conversation with Will. She was nervous because she did not know how the conversation was going to go; not knowing that he was actually anticipating the news.

Taylor was in her bedroom pondering her next move when she heard Chyna exclaim, "Damn that's fucked up." She went into the living room where Chyna was seated in front of the television watching the news; that was her thing. Chyna was one to get upset if she missed the evening news.

"What's wrong Chyna? You good?"

"Then found this guy in the woods naked, gagged, and hands bonded. He was shot in the head. Some execution style type shit for real."

"Damn," Taylor said as she sat on the couch by Chyna.

"I know right."

They watched as the news reporter reported the story.

"The victim, who has been identified as Jerome Bishop, was found by hunters in the woods of Cassatt, SC. We were able to speak to his mother Josephine Bishop. This is her heart felt plea for justice."

Taylor's heart went out to the grieving mother as she pleaded for anyone with information to come forth. She heard the woman say, "Yes, he *was a little rough around the edges, but he was a good boy; my boy."*

A picture of him flashed on the screen. Taylor realized that he was the man that she'd seen at Esquire weeks earlier.

"Holy shit," Taylor said.

"What?"

"I saw that man before."

"What? Where? Shit, when?"

"On the day me and Will went to that bed and breakfast. I saw him at Esquire with Mecco sketchy ass."

"Shit."

"Yeah."

They both sat back on the couch and finished watching the news in silence.

****

Things at Esquire were going well for Will. He sat in his office with an accomplished feeling. He'd taken into account the advice that

Benny gave him about getting out of the game. Shit was getting hot and his heart was no longer in the streets.

His love for hustling had gone. All Will could think about those days was marrying Taylor and her having his baby. He hoped he succeeded in his anniversary impregnation attempt.

Will was in his office looking over the bar receipts from the previous night when Taylor called him.

"Hello my queen," he answered smiling.

"Hey baby. Are you busy?"

"I'm never too busy to talk to you. What's up?"

"We have a situation?"

"A situation? What kind of situation?"

"Well..."

"Well?"

"I'm pregnant," she said nervously.

"That's not a situation baby. That's a blessing," he exclaimed.

"Really?"

"Yes Taylor. Listen to me. I'm not going anywhere. You are going to be my wife. Hell we can get married tomorrow as far as I'm concerned."

"Stop it."

"For real. Let's do it."

"I can't."

"Why?"

"Because it's crazy. My people will flip."

"Okay. Well at least move in with me."

"I'll consider that. Just give me a minute everything's happening so quickly."

"Okay. You think about it and let me know. Let me get back to these receipts. I'll be by your spot when I get done here. I love you Taylor."

"I love you too."

"Woooooo," Will yelled once they hung up. He had gotten up and began dancing when Benny walked in.

"You alright man?" he asked with a sideways glance.

"Bro I'm having a baby."

Benny looked confused.

"Jasmine? You found out the baby was yours?"

"Nah, we both know that baby ain't mine. I'm just playing her game until the kid's born. Taylor's pregnant."

"Damn man, congratulations," he said with a hug. "Y'all making this shit official for real. I'm happy for you dawg."

"Thanks man. Have a seat. I wanted to talk to you anyway. I've been thinking about chillin with that dope boy shit. I especially need to chill with a little jit on the way."

"I think that's a good move. You figured out your exit plan yet?"

"I've put some thought into it. I'm thinking once we move this last kilo of weight I'm done. I know Julio and the Miami gang aren't going to be happy because we've been working together for so long, but fuck um. I got to do what I got to do. The boys ain't gonna like it either, but they'll have to be alright. I just hope there isn't any blow back from it. Know what I mean?"

"Yeah, I feel you. Ain't nothing we can't handle though. When you going to let the crew know?"

"That depends on you and if you're sure you don't want to run it. If you want out too, then I plan on hollering at Tim today and run it by him. See if he wants to take over before I start shutting down anything. Tim is about that money so he'll probably want it. If that's the case then I will have to have a conversation with the crew to inform them of the management change. By any chance that Tim does want out as well, then I'll have Mecco go to the spots and start shutting down."

"That's word. Sounds like a solid plan to me. It's time for us to go legit; I'm out too."

"How are you looking on money?"

"You know I'm straight. I've been putting plans in place for this decision for a while. Plus being part owner of this place is great too. So I got your back on your decision."

"Thanks bro. You've always been there when I needed you. Thicker than thieves..."

"And a lot smarter," Benny added and they chuckled.

"Man we been through some shit."

"Hell yeah. Some real ill shit. So I heard that some fucking hunters found Jerome's body."

"What?"

"Yeah that motherfucker was supposed to be eaten by buzzards before someone even found his bones."

"I hope that shit was clean."

"Of course. You focus on your fine ass future wife and your seed. Me and Mecco got this shit."

"Bet."

"Alright man. I gotta bounce. I'm about to go holla at shorty I met at Buffalo Wild Wings last week."

"Okay now. Don't get too deep in no pussy. Don't forget I need you to cover the club tonight. I'm going to go spend some time with Taylor; probably flowers and dinner. Give her a little reassurance that we're going to be good and I'm happy about the baby."

"Cool. I'll be back by eight."

"Alright bruh," Will said before they gave each other some dap.

"One."

"One."

Will sat behind his desk with his chest poked out feeling confident about his decision.

****

Taylor was happy that the pregnancy conversation went well, but as she laid across the bed all she could think about was Jerome. *Such an awful and humiliating way to die. I hope Will didn't have anything to do with it. What am I going to do? Stop it Taylor. This has nothing to do with you. Mind your business and support your man.*

She decided to take a nap to clear her mind. Unfortunately her nap was brief because images of Jerome's face haunted her dreams.

A knock on her bedroom door startled Taylor out of her restless sleep.

"Come in," Taylor said slowly.

"Hey Tay. Sorry, I didn't know you were sleeping," Sade said as she entered.

"It's okay. What's up?"

"Just checking on you and the little one. How you doing with the whole situation?"

"Better now. I finally told Will and he was actually really supportive. I think everything is going to be alright."

"That's good. You know me and Chyna got your back though, so you're gonna be good; regardless."

"Thanks Shay. What are you about to get into?"

"I met this baller type dude at the mall earlier today. He's taking me to dinner. He's fine than a motherfucker, so I might give him some ass too. Just gotta see how things go."

Taylor laughed and Sade replied with, "What? Bitch don't play. You know you were a hoe just the other day. Hell, I'm surprised Will lasted this long."

They both laughed.

"Stop telling my secrets. Cause you already know..."

"You ain't a hoe unless everybody know," they exclaimed in unison. They laughed at their long used saying.

Chyna came into the room. "What y'all heffas laughing at? Up in here sounding like some cackling hens."

"We're laughing at our trifling whorish ways," Taylor answered.

"Oh lord. I can only imagine how that conversation went," Chyna said with a soft chuckle.

The three of them laid across Taylor's bed and laughed and

talked; something they hadn't done in a while due to their crazy schedules.

****

"What the fuck John? I need you to keep them bartenders in line. Is that too much to ask?"

Will paused and waited for his head bartender, John, to answer.

"No it's not Mr. James."

"Good, I didn't think so. So you let them know that if they enjoy their employment at Esquire, they better fix this shit. Not now but RIGHT now."

"Yes Sir." John quickly exited Will's office.

Will had received several customer complaints about the customer service that they received the prior night. He prided himself on being one of if not the hottest club in Columbia, so anything short of perfection was unacceptable to Will.

Will was packing his brief case to head to Taylor's when his office's direct line rang.

"Hello. Will speaking, how can I help you?"

A man with a dark raspy voice said, "You can help me smile when your bitch ass stop breathing. Pussy ass motherfucker better watch your back because I'm coming for you bitch."

"Oh yeah? Bring it then," Will said before slamming the phone on the receiver. "Bitch ass motherfucker better be ready to bark up this tree," he said as he put his gun in his waist.

When Will left the club that night he never worried or thought twice about the loaded threat.

Chapter 5

"Baby I can't believe I'm already three months."

"I know, you're sexy as hell with that little bump. You're lucky we have to go this doctor's appointment or I'd dirty work you right here."

Taylor laughed. "You're so nasty...I like it though," she said licking her lips.

Will smiled, "You ready baby?"

"Yes."

"Okay come on sexy mama."

Will had grabbed the door knob of Taylor's apartment when his phone rang.

"Yeah," he said. "What?" he paused as the person on the other line explained. "Fuck! Go ahead and call the police. I'm on my way to the doctor with Taylor. I'll be there as soon as I can."

Taylor watched Will's troubled face with concern.

"What is it?"

"Someone broke into the club and vandalized it. Shit! Shit!

Shit!"

Taylor moved to him to comfort him.

"Well babe, you can go ahead and handle that. I'll be alright to go to the appointment alone."

"No, I don't want to miss anything."

Taylor grabbed Will's hand, "Babe you've been great. You've been to every appointment this far. You can't tell me that you don't want to be there. That's your business, your livelihood. I understand. I promise it's okay for you to go."

Will stood there looking unsure.

Taylor continued, "I'll call you as soon as I'm done. Okay?"

"Okay. I love you."

"Love you too babe."

They kissed and Taylor went to her appointment.

"Good day Ms. Jones. How are you feeling today?"

"Hi Doctor Meyers. My morning sickness has finally stopped, so I'm great. How are you today?"

"I'm good. Thanks for asking. Is daddy not joining us today?"

"No. Unfortunately he had an emergency he had to take care of."

"I hope everything is okay."

"It will be."

"Okay. Well let's get you on the table and get you measured," she said as she helped Taylor up from the chair. "I'm thinking we'll do an ultrasound also to check the little one out. If we're lucky we might get a glimpse of the private parts."

"Yay," Taylor said excitedly.

She knew Will would hate that he missed that so she decided to go see him afterwards versus calling him.

****

Will stood in awe as he looked around his club. Tables were broken and tossed, almost all the liquor bottles were smashed on the floor, and the word "Bitch" was spray painted on the wall. *Damn,* he thought as his emotions cycled from sadness to anger.

Will worked with the police officer to complete the report and then met with Benny, Tim, and Mecco in his office.

"I need to find out who did this. Immediately," he said shaking his fist. "I...we worked too hard to get where we are for some cunts to fuck over it. Motherfuckers done got out of line."

"Yeah. This is definitely fucked up," Benny said.

"Yeah bro," Tim added.

"I'm on it boss," Mecco said with an intense stare.

Will knew that Mecco wouldn't stop until he got word of who was behind the vandalism. A brief calm came over Will.

"Alright y'all. Let me know if you hear something. Give me some time to clear my head. I'll holla at you fellas later."

Once the guys left Will's mind was flooded with many thoughts. He knew that a number of people had it out for him. He'd gotten a lot of slack in the streets when he stopped slinging dope. For some reason people had forgotten that Bam liked to bam and had bodies under his belt to prove it. It pissed him off thinking about it. Ever since Will met Taylor he'd been in a constant internal battle with the man he used to be as he attempted to be the man he knew Taylor deserved. He knew he HAD to do better for her and the family they were building together.

Will fixed himself a stiff drink and sat at his desk. He had just placed the cold glass on his temple to calm the ache that had crept in, when Taylor came in.

"Baby are you okay," she asked concernedly.

Will looked up and said, "Hey babe. Just getting a little headache. What you doing here? I thought you were going to call me when you were done at the doctor's."

"I was but I had such good news that I decided to come and share it instead."

"Okay," Will said slowly.

"Well...Doctor Meyers did an ultrasound today-"

"Damn! I missed it. I knew I should have went with you."

"It's okay baby, she set up another one next month."

Taylor kissed the pouting Will.

"You're so cute when you pout," she said with a smirk.

Will forced a smile. "You're the only woman who's ever got me to pout and I'd deny it if I had to," he said playfully.

"Okay Mr. Denial. Well, I have pictures of our little peanut."

"Word?"

"Yep," Taylor said with eyes that sparkled and gleamed.

Taylor watched with excitement as Will looked at the series of picture. When Will got to the final picture he let out a "Whoa". He smiled harder than Taylor ever seen him smile before.

"It's a boy," he exclaimed as he snatched Taylor up in a kiss.

Though Will would have been happy either way, he'd wanted it to be a boy. He'd always wanted a son. Jasmine delivered a healthy baby boy but just as Will suspected he was not the father.

In that moment none of the events of that day mattered.

"We have to celebrate," he said.

****

To celebrate, Will and Taylor went to one of Taylor's favorite restaurants, California Dreaming. Taylor had been on cloud nine ever since her doctor's appointment. She'd been happier than she'd ever been. Her faith in love had finally returned.

"So babe I've been thinking about what you've said before about me needing to stop over thinking things and sometimes I just need to do it. Well, I decided I will move in with you."

"Really?"

"Yes and I would like to get married before we have the baby."

"I'm so happy right now. You've made my night. Let's go home Mrs. James."

Mrs. James has a nice ring to it, Taylor thought as they got up and went to Will's car.

They had left the downtown area and were cruising down the dark road just before Will's sub division when the BMW was rammed from behind. Taylor yelled out in fear.

"What the fuck," Will blurted out while he held the steering wheel firmly.

Taylor braced her hand on the dashboard as they were rammed again.

The second ram was just before a curve. The car ran off the road and smashed into a tree. The windshield shattered. Will's face slammed into the deployed airbag while Taylor's head hit the passenger side window. Pain shot throughout her body. Taylor heard Will moan with pain from the driver's seat.

Taylor was dazed and confused when she heard a faint voice say, "Bitch ass motherfucker. Told you I was coming for you. This is for Jerome." Taylor heard a loud pop and felt wetness on her face. She freaked when she realized the wetness was Will's blood. She passed out from the shock of what had happened.

****

Taylor could hear voices around her.

"Man it's fucked up."

"Yeah. She's going to take it hard."

"I know. We got to have her back for real."

"I know. Three musketeers; all for one and one for all."

"Always."

"Ms. Julia and Mr. Bryant should be here soon."

"That's good. She needs as much support as possible right now."

Taylor slowly opened her eyes to see Chyna and Sade beside her bed.

"Fuck," she whispered. She could barely move and she had a headache from hell.

"Taylor," Chyna and Sade said.

"Where am I?"

"You're in the hospital," Chyna said.

"The hospital?"

"Yeah," Sade confirmed.

"Wait…Will," Taylor yelled as the events of the night flashed through here brain.

Taylor attempted to sit up. In her failed attempt she looked down and noticed her baby bump was no longer there. The heart monitor that she was hooked up to began beeping at an accelerated rate.

"No…no…no," Taylor repeated through tears.

Sade slipped out of the room and grabbed the doctor to help with Taylor's melt down. When Sade, the doctor, and the nurse got back to the room Taylor was sweating and sobbing. The nurse administrated medication into Taylor's IV and exited as the doctor attempted to calm Taylor.

"Hello Ms. Jones, I'm Doctor Lyons. I know you have a lot of questions, but I need for you to try to calm down. Your body has been through trauma on tonight."

"My baby…Will…No."

"My deepest sympathy Ms. Jones, but you truly have to calm down."

"My fiancé. Is he okay? I want to see him."

"I would rather like to speak about you and you injuries first. You have two bruised ribs and a mild concussion. In addition to those injuries unfortunately you had a miscarriage. I'm truly sorry."

Taylor began to cry. "Doctor, where is my fiancé? Is he okay?"

Dr. Lyons looked at Chyna and took a deep breath.

"I hate to be the one to inform you that he's deceased. I was informed that now that you are awake the police are on the way to get your statement."

Taylor had no words to say. Her happiness was snatched all at once. Tears flowed like a river out of her eyes. Chyna and Sade sat by her side helplessly, fighting their own tears.

There was a soft knock on the door that broke up the awkwardness in the room. The nurse reentered the room with two police officers.

"Dr. Lyons these gentlemen are here to speak with Ms. Jones," the nurse stated.

"Very well. Ms. Jones feel free to buzz the nurse's station if you need anything," Dr. Lyons said.

Taylor nodded her head. Dr. Lyons and the nurse exited the room.

"Hello Ms. Jones. I'm Detective Tyson and this is Corporal White. We're the investigating officers on your fiancé's case. We're sorry for your loss and will do all we can to locate the person or persons responsible. So can you tell me what happened just before the crash," Detective Tyson said as Corporal White pulled out a notebook and tape recorder.

Taylor took a deep breath and started with her recollection of the night, "Will and I went to California Dreaming to celebrate...our family."

Taylor paused and cried.

"It's okay Ms. Jones. Take your time," Detective Tyson said.

Chyna handed Taylor a Kleenex and she wiped the tears and snot from her face.

Taylor sniffled and continued, "We ate dinner and had a wonderful evening. I'd just told him that I'd move in with him and we left to go home. We'd just gotten onto Clemson Road when a car hit us in the back. Will fought to maintain control of the car, which he did until the car hit us again. We hit a tree, light post, or something. There was glass everywhere. I was dazed; I guess from hitting the window. I heard Will moan and say my name. Before I could focus enough to respond or move I heard a man say, 'I told you I was coming for you. This is for Jerome'. Then I heard a gun go off. That is all I remember before waking up here."

"Thank you Ms. Jones. I have a few questions about your statement. Did you get a look at the car? Could you tell if it was a car or truck?"

"No. All I saw was the lights."

"Okay, that's good. Do you recall if the lights were low like a car's lights would be or higher like a truck or SUV?"

Taylor paused briefly and said, "It was a truck. I remember being blinded by the light when I looked back."

"Good," Detective White said with a head nod. "My final question is in reference to the statement 'This is for Jerome'. Do you know a Jerome or what that could be about?"

Taylor knew exactly what it was about. She was loyal to Will and she would never speak about it while he was living but she knew she had to in his death.

"Actually I do. I believe the Jerome he was talking about was the man that was found naked and tied up in Cassatt a few months ago. Will had some type of dealings with Jerome. I saw him at Will's club before he was killed."

"Ms. Jones do you think your fiancé had anything to do with that murder?"

"Honestly I do not know, but I think whoever took Will's life did."

"Thank you so much Ms. Jones. You get some rest and we'll get out of your hair. Here's my card if you remember anything else or need my assistance."

"Good night folks," Corporal White added before they exited the room.

Taylor's medication kicked in and she drifted off to sleep. Her sleep started off peaceful. It was around two a.m. when Taylor began to toss and turn. She replayed the accident in dreamland. Taylor got to the point where she was sitting in the seat after the crash. Her eyelids fluttered quickly as she anticipated the gun shot, but it never happened. Instead she was comforted by Will's voice.

"Be strong Tay. It's going to be alright baby. I will always be with you, in your heart where I belong. I love you my sweet, sweet Taylor. What we shared was special. No one or nothing can take that from us; not even death."

Taylor felt the touch of Will's lips on hers. She opened her eyes. Taylor looked around the hospital room. Chyna and Sade were replaced in their chairs by her aunt and uncle. Taylor had never been happier to see them. She laid there drunk in the lingering feeling of Will's kiss. She closed her eyes and drifted back to sleep.

****

"I can't believe this shit man! My motherfucking dog is gone!" Benny yelled through drunken tears. "This shit can't be happening." Benny buried his face in his hands.

Tim and Mecco also sat in the office of Esquire during Benny's rant; eyes blood shot. They were all in a meeting when Benny had received the call about the accident from Will's next door neighbor.

Benny, Tim, and Mecco high tailed it to the scene. When they got there Taylor had already been taken to the hospital and the coroner was on site for Will's body. Benny felt like he was watching a movie as he was watched the police place Will into the body bag. That image forever would be edged in his brain, but he tried desperately to numb the pain with Vodka.

Chapter 6

Taylor's hospital stay was a short one. She was released shortly after three p.m. the following afternoon. Julia and Bryant did all that they knew to do to help Taylor hold it together.

They'd gotten her to her apartment and into bed. Julia sat on the bed next to Taylor and stroked her hair.

"Is there anything I could do for you Pumpkin?" Julia asked.

"No. I'm okay."

"Are you sure?"

"Yes ma'am."

"Okay. Here's your remote. I'll be out in the living room with your uncle. Call me if you need me," Julia said before she kissed Taylor on the forehead.

"Would you lay with me? At least until I fall asleep."

"Of course Virtue."

Taylor smiled. No one but Julia ever called her Virtue. They laid in silence and watched *The Fresh Prince of Bel-Air.*

Taylor tried to focus on the show but her thoughts circled

around all the things she needed to do; call Will's mom, get her things from Will's house, and return the baby's things. Sadly Taylor looked at her engagement ring. The item that signified love and commitment just days prior had become a reminder of hurt and pain.

****

Benny went with Will's mother to identify the body; by far the hardest thing he'd ever done. The medical examiner had a sheet wrapped around his head to cover the gunshot wound. He fought hard to be strong for Will's mother as he looked at his friend, his brother, on the table. Benny was broken inside, but he knew he had to maintain. There was no time for Benny to lose focus; he was all she had at that point.

"Mama Janet come sit down," he said to her after exiting the autopsy room.

"I can't believe he's gone Benny," she said through tears.

"He was all I had. My only boy."

"You have me Mama Janet. You've been my mother when mine wasn't around. Will was more than just my friend, he was my family. Just like you. I'm going to help you get through this Ma."

"Thank you Benny," she whispered before burying her face into his chest.

Benny wiped a tear as he embraced Janet. He thought of Taylor at that moment. He knew she had to have been a mess and planned to see about her as well.

I got you bro, he thought to himself as he visualized Will giving him a head nod.

****

"Don't fucking play with me Dirk. I will bash your shit in," Mecco said looking at the bonded man that sat in the chair in front of him.

"Fuck you," Dirk said as he spat in Mecco's face.

Mecco reared back and connected his fist to Dirk's face.

"No bitch. Fuck you."

Mecco continued to hit Dirk until he had just about lost consciousness.

He got right up to Dirk's ear and whispered, "You got heart, but listen closely. I know you know who was behind what went down with Bam. I respect your loyalty to the streets but check this out. I know I'm probably going to have to kill you, but I'm not going to do it just yet. First, I'm going to go to your baby mama house, fuck her real good, tie her up, fuck your daughter, and then bring their heads to you. See if that'll make you talk. If that ain't enough, next stop would be by your mama and sister."

"Fuck man," Dirk slurred through his swelling lip. "My motherfucking family?"

"What's it going to be, you or you and them? I don't give a fuck either way. So the choice is yours, and by that I mean start fucking talking now."

Defeated, Dirk began to speak, "Red got wind that you and your crew did Jerome. Quickest way to kill a snake is chop his head off, so Bam pussy ass had to get dealt with. Your ass will be next," he added with a laugh.

"That's fine but not before you," Mecco said as he pulled a flask from his jacket pocket. He opened it and poured the contents on Dirk.

"What the fuck? Is that gas?" he asked trying to free his zip tied hands.

Mecco smiled at the sight of him wiggling in the chair.

"Don't bitch up now. All that shit you were just talking."

"Ain't no bitch in me. You'll get yours; really soon too."

Mecco struck a match, "I'll see you in hell then."

He threw the match on Dirk. Dirk screamed out with pain. Mecco watched him squirm; enjoying every minute of it. The screaming stopped and Mecco moved toward the door of the house. He pulled out his phone and called Benny.

"Yo, Red's behind that shit; payback for his crab ass brother...Yeah, I took care of Dirk's ass."

He paused at the door while Benny quickly ran down their next move.

"Bet. I'll meet you at the club," he said as he walked out of Dirk's trap house.

He'd made it to the step of the house when he was shot in the back of the head.

"What the fuck was that?" Benny asked from the other side of the phone.

"Mec. Mecco. Yo, what's going on?"

The gunman picked up Mecco's phone and said, "What happened is his brains are exposed. Two down and two to go; I'll be seeing you and Tim bitch asses soon. Watch your back pretty boy."

"Fuck you. You-"

The man hung up on Benny and his rant. Benny was furious and sailed his cell phone at the wall in Will's office.

"Fuck!" he yelled.

****

Taylor had an outer body experience during Will's funeral. She sat there puffy eyed looking at his memorial photo beside the coffin. Due to Will's wound, the funeral was closed casket.

Taylor's family and friends were there supporting her. Sade and Chyna sat on the opposite sides of her; each holding a hand. Julia and Bryant sat directly behind her; Julia rubbed Taylor's shoulders and back throughout the service.

Though Taylor was hurting like nobody's business because of Will's unexpected death, she also had the feeling of confusion present in her mind. Benny told Taylor about Mecco being found at Dirk's house shot and burned. It was too much happening too soon. She decided to go back to Beaufort after the funeral. She needed to get away. For all she knew, her surviving was a fluke and someone may come after her.

Taylor was almost totally numb by sadness by the time they left the burial site. She said her goodbyes to Janet and Benny.

"You take care of yourself Taylor. I'm here for you if you ever need anything," Benny said sincerely.

"Thanks Benny."

"I'm serious Taylor. I made a promise to Bam to make sure you were straight if anything happened to him."

What kind of shit was Will into to feel the need to make Benny promise something like that? Taylor thought as she stared at Benny.

"Oh yeah," Benny said as he reached into his coat pocket. He pulled out an envelope and handed it to Taylor.

"What is this?"

"It's a little something Bam had set aside for you and," he hesitated, "the baby."

Taylor's eyes went to the ground sadly.

"It's ten thousand in that envelope along with documentation leaving you Bam's half of the club."

"What? Benny I can't-"

"Yes you can. Bam loved you. I'd never seen him so in love. You were special to him so you're special to me. Know I'm always here for you. Don't matter where or when; I got your back."

Taylor hugged Benny, wiped her eyes, and walked to Julia and Bryant's car. She left Columbia that day and didn't look back.

Chapter 7

Though Beaufort was not where Taylor wanted to be prior to Will's murder, it was where she needed to be after. Julia supported her through her grieving process. Taylor had no worries. She spoke to Chyna and Sade regularly so she remained in the know with them. Benny kept his word to Will and ensured Taylor was taken care of. Every month Benny would send Taylor between fifteen hundred and five thousand dollars. No one knew about her building fortune; not Julia or Bryant or Chyna or Sade.

Taylor refused to let the money change her. She went to school online to finish her Bachelors of Science in Business Administration with emphasis in accounting while she worked part time at a check to cash agency.

The money came like clockwork for a year and then it stopped. The first month Taylor didn't think anything of it. By the second month she'd gotten curious so she called Sade.

"Hey Shay."

"What up Tay?"

"Shit. Ain't nothing."

"I feel you. It's about the same here. What you been up to?"

"Just working and trying to get finished with school. This semester is half way through, and then I only have one more semester. Thank the lord."

"That's what's up. I'm proud of you. You could have easily given up once Will died but you didn't. You're fucking amazing."

"Thanks Shay."

"You're welcome."

"Yo. Have you seen Benny lately?"

"Nah. Why what's up?"

"He'd been checking on me once a month or so and I hadn't heard anything lately. That's it."

"Oh. I was planning on going out to the club tomorrow for lady's night. I'll holla at Tim."

"Alright. So how things going for y'all? I miss you and Chyna so much."

"Chyna has been working harder than usually at school. Graduation is in two weeks. You still coming right?"

"Yes, I think I've been away from Columbia long enough. Plus it wouldn't hurt to check out the club. It still blows me that I own half of it."

"I bet it does. I don't know why you're working at that check to cash joint when you own part of one of the hottest clubs in Columbia. I'd be cashing in on that shit."

"You know that's not what I want to do. I only have one more semester to get my degree so that's my focus. Y'all still planning to make that move to Atlanta."

"Yeah. I've contacted a few salons and Chyna's been trying to get on at a clinic. You still going to come cause I think Chyna might flake?"

"Why you say that?"

"Her and Brian done got real cozy over the past year."

"We've been planning this for years so I don't think that'll matter."

"She on that planning her imaginary wedding type shit," Sade added with a laugh.

"Well damn," Taylor said laughing. "Well I'm still down for moving. You know I've out grown Beaufort years ago."

"I feel you. Alright chick I'ma holla at you later. I have a shopping date."

"Alright girl. Later."

"Later."

****

Benny laid in the bed reflecting on his life. The Streets had finally caught up with him. One night as he stepped out of his car at his house he was struck by a bat.

When Benny went down he was hit and kicked repeatedly by several men. He laid on the ground in and out and consciousness. They robbed him of the five grand he'd taken out of the safe that night to send to Taylor the next day.

The master mind behind the attack was Red. He'd come to bring truth to his threat. Red had the bat and was about to bash Benny's head to the ground. Lucky for Benny his neighbor drove up at that moment. The guys fled around the corner to their waiting vehicle and the neighbor called 911.

A little over a month later and Benny laid in the hospital hanging on by a thread. He'd had multiple strokes and his body was immobile. *I knew things would come to this. I should have pushed harder to get Bam to see that we needed to get out the game. Now I'm laying here in a hospital alone. Bam and Mecco's dead. Fuck. Hope I go ahead and die soon, this is not the way to live,* Benny thought as a tear fell from his eye.

****

"Tay."

"Yeah," Taylor said half asleep.

"You up?"

"Fuck no," she paused and looked at the clock. "It's three in the morning."

"I know. I couldn't wait to tell you this."

"What is it Shay?"

"So I went to lady's night at Esquire like I told you. It was off the hook by the way. But anyways. I talked to Tim and he told me that Benny's in the hospital."

"What? What happened?"

"Some motherfuckers beat him half to death. Literally."

"Damn."

"He's been in the hospital for like a month. Tim's been running the club. Will's crew is getting taken out one by one. What the fuck is going on Tay?"

"I don't know what all Will was into, but it seems like some heavy shit. Keep me posted if you hear anything else. I'm going to visit him when I come down."

"Okay. Good night."

"Good night."

Taylor could not go back to sleep. She pondered over Sade's question of "what was going on".

****

Thank you God, Benny thought as he felt the life leaving his body.

"Code blue, room two C..."

The nurses and doctors rushed around Benny's room in attempted to resuscitate him. The doctor looked at his watch and said, "Notify the next of kin that Mr. Gray passed at eight fifty-seven p.m."

He walked out of the room while the nurses disconnected Benny from the machines and covered him up.

****

Just before Taylor went to Columbia for Chyna's graduation she was contacted by Benny's attorney, Mr. Blackwell. He'd informed her of his death and that she had become the sole owner of Esquire. Mr. Blackwell also mentioned that there had been an investor interested in the club since Will's death if selling was an option for her. Benny had been totally against it because it was his way of paying homage to Will. Taylor on the other hand wanted to put Columbia in her past so she expressed that she had no desire to keep the club.

Taylor was ready to start over. She'd decided that when she went to Atlanta that she wanted her own shit; she did not want to rent. Selling the club would provide her the immediate means to do that.

Taylor met with Mr. Blackwell when she went to Columbia.

"Good afternoon Ms. Jones."

"Hello."

"Glad you could make our meeting. Please have a seat. Would you like some water, soda, or juice?"

"No thank you."

"Very well. Onto business. Since our conversation I've been in contact with the potential buyers. They have made an offer of three hundred and fifty thousand dollars. I'm not a real estate agent but I believe that is low for the square footage of the building. Plus it's in an ideal location. So there is room for negotiation."

"I'm not interested in a lot of back and forth negotiations. Tell them they have a deal for three hundred and seventy five thousand. Take it or leave it."

"Are you sure you don't want to go a little higher?"

"Yes I'm sure."

Taylor had been house hunting and found a two bedroom town home in an Atlanta up and coming neighborhood near downtown Atlanta. The list price was two hundred seventy thousand dollars. She figured she could do any upgrades as well as furniture purchases with the additional one hundred thousand dollars she'd have left.

"Yes ma'am. I will contact the buyer and make it happen."

"Great," Taylor said as she got up and shook Mr. Blackwell's hand.

"I almost forgot Ms. Jones. Mr. Gray also left instructions for me to give you the contents of Esquire's safe."

Mr. Blackwell handed Taylor a bronze and gold box. She was eager to know what was in there but she decided to wait until she got in her car.

"Thank you again Mr. Blackwell. I'll be in touch."

Once in her car Taylor opened the box. The contents included almost eight thousand dollars in cash, Will's title to his car, and most importantly a ring box that contained her and Will's wedding bands. Taylor was ambushed by emotions. She sat in her car for almost thirty minutes and cried before she left and went to Chyna and Sade's apartment.

She was so happy to see Chyna and Sade.

"I'm so proud of you Chyna. In a few hours you'll be walking across that stage."

"Thanks Tay. I can't believe it. It felt like this day would never come."

"I feel you. Wish I was walking with you today. But my day's coming soon."

"All that matters is that you do it."

"Yeah. I love you guys."

"I love you too."

"Y'all bitches need to gone somewhere with all that sappy shit," Sade interjected as she came from the kitchen.

Taylor and Chyna laughed before telling her to shut up in unison.

"Whatever. Y'all hoes be getting all sensitive and shit. So what about this move though?"

"I don't know. I haven't heard anything back from that clinic yet. But Brian's been talking about us getting married. Being an Army wife wouldn't be that bad. Only thing with that is he's here for at least another two years then I don't know where we'd go."

"Wow," Taylor said.

Sade shook her head and said, "What about you Tay?"

"I'm still going. I got these last six classes to get done. My plan is to be there by the end of the year. Got some things working. What's your plan?"

"I'm going. I found a salon in downtown Atlanta that I'm really digging. I'm going up there next week to check some things out. My plan is to be there by the end of summer cause our lease here runs out in August."

"That's what's up," Taylor said. "So, I've decided to sell the club."

"What?"

"No."

"Yeah. I ain't got no time for no club. I've been looking at a town home in Atlanta that I'd like to buy, so I think it's a good trade off."

"Well, you know I support whatever you decide to do," Chyna said.

"Thank you love."

"That's cool I guess," Sade said rolling her eyes. "So what's the move before graduation? We gonna eat or what? A bitch is hungry."

"Shit. Me too," Taylor cosigned.

"Y'all bitches always hungry," Chyna said laughing. "Mom, grandma, and Aunt Betty are on their way now; they should be here in about thirty minutes. They are bringing some food; red rice, chicken, macaroni, pasta salad, and banana pudding. Dad and his new wife are supposed to come so we might go eat afterwards so it's whatever y'all want to do."

"Shit, we can do both," Sade said.

"Yep, cause Ms. Toni know she be throwing down," Taylor added. "So how's things going with your pops?"

"He's been doing better. I still don't put too much faith in his words though. Lately he's been on trying to buy me. It's not going to work, but I'm not gonna pass up his gifts. That's for damn sure."

"Don't blame you there," Taylor said.

Sade turned on some music and said, "Let's get this party started. Time to get cute. Show these hoes how Beaufort girls do."

"Fo sho," Chyna and Taylor exclaimed.

They danced around and had a good time. The three musketeers were united again. That night was the last night they spent together for a while.

Chapter 8

Sade and Taylor both made the move to Atlanta. Sade was all the way set up by the time Taylor made it to Atlanta. She'd gotten settled nicely at her salon job and got an apartment in downtown Atlanta. Taylor bought the townhouse that she'd been watching under asking price and started an accounting job at Brown & Brown Law Firm.

Life for the girls was promising. They were all working on the lives they'd talked about as kids. Chyna ended up staying in Columbia. Not only did she and Brian get married but they were also expecting a baby. Though Sade and Taylor gave her a hard time they were happy for her.

Taylor and Sade's lifestyle quickly adapted to the hustle and bustle of city life. Their schedules conflicted so they did not spend as much time together as they'd initially planned so one day they put time aside and planned a spa day.

Taylor drove her new Honda Accord (she retired her Civic prior to the move) over to Sade's apartment. Sade greeted Taylor looking fresh in a fitted tank, tennis skirt, and Coach sneakers. They hugged briefly.

"Now don't you look cute. You done changed your style on me?"

"You like?" Sade asked as she posed.

"I do. You pull off the country club look well."

Taylor looked around the apartment. It looked totally different than it did a few months prior when Taylor was last there.

"You've made some upgrades since I've been here."

"Yeah. I had to do a little something-something."

"A little something-something? Looks like you trying to get on *MTV Cribs*; white couches, sculptures, and a flat screen. It's nice but I just don't want you to go in debt trying to be like the other flashy Atlanta folks."

"You always worrying."

"Hell, one of us have to."

"I'm good. I'll tell you about it on our way to the spa. You driving or you want me to drive?"

"It don't matter."

"How about I drive so I can show you my new car."

"You got a new car too?"

"Yep. Let's go."

Taylor was curious to how Sade was able to afford all those things. *She must got her a good sugar daddy,* she thought as Sade locked up.

Taylor followed Sade through the parking garage to a black

Mustang.

"Here's my baby," she said smiling from ear to ear.

"Nice Shay. What the hell are you doing? You done found you a rich man?"

Sade laughed, "Actually I've found some rich men."

"Oh damn," Taylor said looking at Sade sideways.

"Get in and I'll tell you."

Sade told Taylor about one of her clients Sylvia. "Sylvia always came in the shop fly. I'd hear her on the phone making appointments and what nots. I could tell she was someone important. One day I asked her what she did. Her response blew me at first. She said 'I provide companionship to the upper class'. I was confused and she told me she ran an escort service."

"She's a pimp, Madame, whatever they call them?"

"Not quite. She's not selling prostitutes. Escorts provide company for the clients. Sex is optional though."

"So that's what you've been doing?"

"Yes. Once I grilled Sylvia she invited me to check her business out. I went that night, watched her, and mingled with the girls. It was cool and the caliber of guys she caters to is crazy; business owners, lawyers, politicians, and celebrates. I've been on some amazing dates with no strings attached. Not to mention the money is good. I get paid between five hundred and a thousand dollars per event and it's an additional upfront payment of five hundred dollars if we agree on sex."

"Damn."

"Yeah. I'm still at the salon because I enjoy doing hair, but that's only pocket change. I'm trying to set myself up."

"I hope you're being smart and not blowing all the money. You need to invest. Make your money work for you."

"I don't know nothing about investing."

"Ding dong your best friend works money and numbers every day. I didn't tell anyone, but at Will's funeral Benny gave me ten thousand dollars. I took that money and invested it. I've almost doubled it."

"No bullshitting?"

"Nah."

"I knew that your big head would work for you one day," Sade said laughing.

"Fuck you. With a hard one," Taylor said joining her in laughter.

The girls went to the spa and enjoyed their day of relaxation.

****

Over time Taylor helped Sade manage her finances while Sade managed to attempt to recruit Taylor every chance she got. Taylor was in a good place and wanted no parts of the escort life.

For the most part Taylor was content with her life. She'd been in an ongoing relationship with a young man named Donte. Other than minor issues, they were doing well.

It was a week before Taylor's twenty fifth birthday when all hell broke loose.

Taylor went to Savannah, Georgia for a three day conference for her job. The presenter got food poisoning while at dinner on the second day so they were released early. Taylor decided to surprise Donte. She'd stopped to her house, grabbed her sexy lingerie, stilettos, and wine. Her intent was to be laid out on his bed looking delicious when he got home.

Taylor sang the whole way to Donte's. When she pulled up to his apartment, to her surprise his car was in the parking lot. *Damn. He must have got off early. Oh well.*

Taylor grabbed her bag and walked up to the door. She inserted her key and walked into the apartment. She closed the door and immediately heard the sounds of intense sex coming from the bedroom. *I know good and damn well this motherfucker ain't in here fucking some bitch!*

Taylor put the bag down and went straight to the bedroom. She opened the door and stood in shock not believing what was before her eyes. Donte was fucking alright, just not the "bitch" Taylor expected.

Donte was on the bed deep in some ass; literally. He was doing another man from behind. Taylor watched while Donte clinched the guy's ass cheeks as he drilled his dick deep inside of him. Donte was so focused on what he was doing that he did not see Taylor standing there.

"Fuck, I'm about to cum babe. Hope you're ready," Donte said.

"No bitch I hope you're ready," Taylor exclaimed.

Donte and his boy toy both jumped. Donte quickly pulled out and started to explain.

"Fuck you and your explanation," she said as she headed to the door.

The boy toy quickly got his things and started getting dressed.

Taylor was enraged. She went outside to her car and grabbed her Louie Ville Slugger out of her trunk. The mystery man slid passed her while she was at her car. With her heart racing fast and her temple pulsating she reentered the apartment.

Taylor took the bat to any and everything she could; to include Donte. She destroyed just about everything in his apartment then rendered him a huge "Fuck you" before she left.

Once Taylor got into her car she called Sade.

"Hello."

"Shay you won't fucking believe what this motherfucker did."

"What? What happened?"

"First off I found out why our sex life had been going downhill. Why his dick wouldn't stay hard."

"Calm down Tay. What happened?"

"I just walked in on Donte fucking a dude."

"What? Get the fuck out of here. I can't believe that shit."

"Yep. Straight ball smacking with a motherfucking dude."

"Fuck. What you going to do?"

"Say fuck all this love bullshit and get this money with you."

"Bet. As long as you're sure."

"Yeah I'm sure, but first get some bail money ready cause the police may be after me in a few."

Virtually
CHALLENGED
AN ESCORT'S STORY
2
NATIONAL BESTSELLING AUTHOR
J. ASMARA

Prologue

Still in the bathroom…

Taylor replayed the conversation she heard in the hotel suite as she laid in the tub.

"Tony is tired of you dodging him Al. You didn't even tell him you were coming into town. He got to hear it in the streets. Here you are around here renting bitches, going on trips, and wearing tailor suits and shit. Rumor has it that you're even in the pimp business now. Where's Tony's fucking money?"

"Fuck this shit! Vince I don't have no patience for this muthafucka. He ain't about to come up off Tony's money. Let me do this worm."

"Calm the fuck down, Bobby. The boss gave me instructions on how to handle this matter. Timing is everything little brother, but you can be the one to do him in when the time comes."

Taylor knew she did not want to meet Vince nor Bobby. She laid in the tub thinking of the shoulda, woulda, couldas of the situation. *Only if I stuck to my guns and said no to this job. I knew better*, she thought.

Albert was getting smacked around pretty bad from what Taylor could hear. She grabbed the twenty-two she had in her purse and prayed. *Lord I know that I've been slacking on our time together but please don't let me die. Lord please.* Taylor was zoned out until she heard Vince near the bathroom door.

"Bobby let me drain my main then we can get out of here."

Fuck, she thought as she held onto the gun tightly.

Chapter 1

Being an escort was never on Taylor Virtue Jones' list of future endeavors, but life always had a way of turning the tables. Finding the third, and last if she had her way, man that she'd ever fallen in love with in bed with another man was the final straw. Taylor had heard about the rise of men on the down low but she never suspected Donte to be one of those men.

Taylor had spent a few hours in jail for her expression of her emotions before her childhood friend Sade bailed her out. Those few hours weren't ideal for Taylor but they were warranted after the destruction she caused.

Taylor busted Donte's apartment as well as his ribs with a bat during her tangent. As far as Taylor was concerned Donte was lucky she grabbed the bat out of the trunk and not the nine millimeter that was in the glove box. It cost her a little money and a year of probation, but Taylor didn't care. That was how she got into the business. So in her mind it was worth it. Catching Donte's bitch ass with that dude changed her life.

Taylor and Sade met with the "Misses" of the *Exquisite Evenings* escort service Sylvia, two days after the Donte incident.

"Nice to finally meet you," Sylvia said. It was evident to Taylor that Sade had spoken of her often. Taylor glared at Sade who smiled and shrugged her shoulders.

"Nice to meet you as well," Taylor said as Sylvia showed her around her home.

You'd never think that the mansion that sat in the well to do subdivision in Atlanta Georgia was the nucleus of a well devised operation. Sylvia really impressed Taylor and right then and there she made up her mind to learn the business inside and out.

"Well beautiful if you are ready, I will set you up with a date tomorrow. The gentleman's name is Alex Grimes. He's a doctor at Northside Hospital. You will be accompanying him to an investor's banquet. Can you handle that?"

"Yes ma'am."

"Alright, no street shit. I'm about my money and I'm putting my name out there, so don't make me regret it."

"Okay," Taylor said looking at the seriousness in Sylvia's face.

"Good. Since this is your first job I will furnish your attire. After this you are on your own. Understood?"

"Yes."

"I will also have someone to do your makeup. I'm all for natural beauty but I'm not in a normal business with "normal" people. The date is at eight. I want you here by six."

"Yes."

"Okay. Go now," Sylvia said with a wave of the hand. Taylor liked Sylvia's boss attitude.

****

The banquet was on a Saturday so Taylor had all day to prepare mentally and physically. She started her day with a jog and then went to the spa for a facial, massage, manicure, and pedicure.

The closer to six it got the more nervous Taylor got. *Can I really do this? I've let Sade hype me up to do this. Stop over thinking this Taylor. Hell, go on a few dates and stack some money. Breathe...* She thought before she took a deep breath.

Taylor forgot about her concerns once she got to Sylvia's. She had a room designated for her "newbies". There were racks filled with dresses, shoes, handbags, and jewelry. Taylor was dressed in a long coral dress, gold jewelry, and gold shoes. Once her makeup was done Taylor felt like a million bucks.

"Hello Virtue," she said as she smiled at her reflection in the full length mirror.

At seven-fifteen there was a black Lincoln Continental to pick Taylor up.

"Good evening ma'am," the driver said as he opened the door. "I'm Stephon and I will be your driver for the evening."

Once inside the car Stephon informed Taylor that they were going to pick Mr. Grimes up at his home. When they arrived to the house Taylor was surprised that Alex was a good looking mid-forties man. She expected him to be hard on the eyes since he was hiring an escort, but he was actually tall dark and very handsome. *Damn he is fine,* she thought as she watched him walk to the car. Stephon got out of the car to open the door for him.

"Thank you," Alex said to Stephon as he got into the car. He smiled when he saw Taylor.

"Hello beautiful. I'm Alex," he said offering his hand.

"Hello Alex. I'm Virtue."

"Virtue, that's a beautiful name for a beautiful woman." Taylor blushed as he kissed her hand.

"Thank you."

They talked the whole way to the banquet. Taylor didn't even feel like she was working by the time they got to the event.

Alex was a complete gentleman. He escorted her around the event on his arm; proudly introducing her to the attendees.

Taylor enjoyed the atmosphere. She knew that was the caliber of lifestyle she wanted. If being a high priced escort would be the means to her end, so be it.

Taylor had a fantastic evening with Alex. He confirmed that he had a good night as well as they walked to the lobby of the banquet hall.

"I've had a lovely time with you Virtue. I'm not ready to end our night yet," he said.

"I've enjoyed myself as well. What do you have in mind?"

"There's a really nice lounge not far from here. Would you like to go?"

"Okay. That sounds fun."

"Great," Alex said showing off the benefits of having a great dental plan.

Once they got to the lounge Alex lead her to a secluded back corner of the building.

"I'm glad you agreed to come with me. I really wanted to spend a little more time with you. "

Taylor looked around trying to take in all of the beauty of the space.

"Pretty nice huh?"

"Yes," she said as she nodded and picked up the menu off of the table. "I need something to drink."

"Whatever you want beautiful."

Taylor smiled because she could see Alex watching her every move. She really enjoyed and appreciated his attentiveness.

A young lady came to their table. "Good evening. I'm April. What can I get for you this evening?"

"I would like some Ciroc on the rocks and whatever this lovely lady wants."

"For you ma'am?"

"I'd like to have a cup of the mint tea and a cup of water with lemon."

"Would that be all?"

"Yes," Taylor said.

"The both of you look very nice."

"Thank you," Taylor and Alex both said.

"And that dress is absolutely beautiful."

"Thank you dear."

"You're welcome. I'll be back with your drinks."

"She's right Virtue. That dress is stunning on you. It looks like it was made just for you."

"Well thank you Alex."

"Tell me something. What are you doing working for Sylvia? You're different from the other ladies."

Hell. How good of a client is he?

"Well honestly, this is my first day. My friend has been working for Sylvia for a little while now. After a few failed attempts of a happily ever after I said the heck with it and here I am."

"I think you're a special woman. I'm glad to be your first date. Sylvia and I have been friends for a long time. With my busy schedule I don't have time to date, so she helps me with the major events I have. So don't think that I'm just hiring women every week to please some nasty desire."

"You don't have to explain anything to me."

"I know that, but I want to. I like you Virtue, and I want to see you again. Hell honestly, if I was not trying to be a perfect gentleman this evening I'd tell you what I'd like to do to you," Alex paused as April returned with their drinks.

"Thank you for being a perfect gentleman."

"I can't promise you that the next time though. I want to see you again. As a matter a fact are you free tomorrow?"

"Wow. Tomorrow? Around what time?"

"Tomorrow evening around six. First before you answer that. Do you like hockey?"

"I'm not familiar with hockey. Only thing I know is that the guys skate around with sticks trying to hit the puck into their opponent's goal."

"Well at least you have the gist of the game. My brother's company has a reserved row at Philips Arena. He doesn't care for hockey so I use his pass. So would you like to go?"

Taylor was always adventurous and liked to experience new things.

"I'd love to."

"Good. I'll give Sylvia a call in the morning to set up our date. I want to ensure you are taken care of."

It was after midnight when they left the lounge. Alex left Taylor with a "good night beautiful" and a kiss on the cheek. Stephon drove her back to Sylvia's where she got her car and went straight home. She showered and went to bed content with her evening.

Sylvia called Taylor the following morning around ten. Taylor had just got in from the gym.

"Hello."

"Hello Taylor. Excuse me, Virtue. This is Sylvia."

"Good morning."

"I was going to call to set up a meeting to talk about your first date, but I received a phone call from Alex that ensured me it went well. He is quite fond of you actually. I think you have your first daddy."

"Daddy?"

"Yes, that is what I call the clients who take a liking to a certain girl. They are the ones who go out of their way to 'keep' the girl. Perks are usually numerous dates, gifts, and hefty tips."

"Oh okay."

"Alex has never 'kept' a girl before so you must be good company. So I was informed that you are to meet him at the Philips Arena this evening. The car service I use is Tip Top Cars. I suggest that my girls never have the guys pick them up from their home; no matter how comfortable you get with one another. This is business. Don't ever forget that. Come by the house at noon. I will have your payment for last night."

"Yes ma'am I'll see you then."

Taylor showered, ate, and relaxed for a while before going to Sylvia's. When Taylor got there Sylvia handed her seventeen hundred dollars. Taylor was both excited and confused. "This is from one night?"

"This is two nights and a tip."

"Two nights? I thought we got paid after the dates."

"Yes usually that's how it's done, to ensure the girls follow through with the commitment. It protects me and the clients; however you are a kept woman now and Alex requested that you to get your money up front for now on. So there you are Ms. Virtue. Shay was right, you're a natural."

"Well thank you Sylvia."

"No thank you. I see us making lots of money together. Word of advice; always keep your daddies happy. If you know what I mean," she said smiling.

"I will remember that."

"Make sure you dress warm for your date tonight," Sylvia added quickly as Taylor left.

Taylor was ecstatic. Her side hustle started to look promising.

Chapter 2

Taylor battled with what to wear on her hockey date. Though it was a sporting event she still had to be sexy. She settled on a pair of fitted jeans, a fitted shirt, blazer and knee high boots. Taylor called the car service and had them drop her off at the arena. Alex was at the ticket booth waiting for her. She watched as his face lit up with every twist of her hips. Taylor was happy with her outfit choice; she matched Alex well in his jeans, t-shirt, sport coat, and Stacy Adams.

"Hello beautiful lady," Alex said greeting Taylor with a tight embrace.

Damn he smells good, she thought as he held her.

"Hello to you handsome," Taylor replied as he kissed her on the cheek.

"Thank you for gracing me with your presence for a second day in a row. I hope you enjoy your first hockey match."

"Thank you for inviting me. I'm actually really excited."

"Good. Let's go."

He grabbed a bag that sat near the ticket booth and they

walked in; hand in hand. He led her to their seats that were two rows away from the player's bench. Taylor was like a kid in a candy store as she took in the experience. The excitement quickly subsided when a chill came over her.

"Are you cold?"

"A little."

"I figured that much," Alex said as he went into the bag and pulled out a throw blanket. He carefully placed it around Taylor's shoulders.

"Hmmm. Thank you," she said gratefully.

Taylor and Alex watched the game with occasional cuddling under the blanket. She enjoyed herself. If it had not been for the stack of money she got from Sylvia, she'd think it was a real date. Taylor and Alex had been so wrapped up in what they had going on, that they didn't realize the last play was made until the final buzzer went off.

"Holy shit. They won," Alex exclaimed. "You must be a lucky charm because we'd lost the first three games of the season."

"So that's why everyone is losing their minds cheering right now?"

"Yeah. It was looking really bad. Hope they keep the momentum so they can have a decent ranking this season. Virtue, is it okay if I'm a little forward with you for a minute?"

Taylor looked at Alex confused as to what brought about that question.

"Sure go ahead."

"I really want to taste you. I've been envisioning my face deep in your pussy ever since last night."

"Wasn't expecting that," Taylor said blushing.

"I hope I didn't offend you but I just wanted you to know. I'm very attracted to you."

"No you're okay. It was just shocking."

"Good. I don't want you to run out of here. So what do you want to do now? Want to get something to eat? Maybe a movie?"

Sylvia's advice popped into her mind. *Keep your daddies happy.* She liked being kept and planned on staying that way.

"How about whatever you'd like that involves you tasting me before or after?"

Alex smiled so hard that Taylor noticed that he had slight dimples in his cheeks.

"Then let's get out of here," he said as he got up and reached for Taylor's hand.

Alex led her to a silver Corvette. "Nice. You didn't strike me as a Corvette guy."

"Was that an old guy joke?" he asked jokingly.

"You are not an old guy, first off. I thought you'd have a more conservative car that's all. This is badass."

"Thanks. I've been in love with Corvettes since I was a small boy. I said when I got a good job I was going to get one. This is actually my second one. I call her Janet."

"Ms. Jackson if you're nasty," Taylor added with a giggle.

"Exactly!" Alex exclaimed.

They got in the car and Alex drove to his house. On the drive he'd filled Taylor in on his plan which was for her to be an appetizer, order delivery food, and watch a movie.

Taylor followed Alex into the house. He shut the door behind Taylor and then kissed her. Before Taylor knew it Alex had backed her to the entry way's wall. Taylor got lost in the intense but sensual way Alex kissed her. She dropped her purse on the floor and wrapped her hands around his head.

Alex caressed her body slowly and unbuttoned her jeans. He slid his hands into her panties and gently pet her kitty. Taylor moaned softly while his mouth was still pressed on hers. Alex played in her wetness as he moved his kisses to her neck.

Taylor anticipated the pleasure his mouth was going to bring. She braced herself on the wall as Alex pulled her jeans down. She looked down at the top of his salt and pepper hair as he kissed her thighs. *Damn that feels nice. He looks like he can eat some good pussy. Please don't disappoint me. It's been a minute since anyone's ate it.*

Alex teased Taylor by kissing her through her panties. Her hips rolled inviting him to sample her nectar. He slid her panties to the side and sucked on her pussy.

"Mmmm," he said before he spread her legs and licked her clit.

Though Taylor's jeans restricted how wide her legs could spread, Alex navigated his way around like a pro. He quickly flicked her clit. Taylor grabbed his head as she came in his mouth. Alex gripped her thighs as he consumed all of her juices. Alex loved how sweet she tasted. *She has to be mine,* Alex thought as he watched Taylor get lost in her orgasm.

Alex grabbed Taylor's panties and ripped them off before burying his head deep between her thighs. Alex's tongue game was serious and Taylor liked it. Taylor was in heaven, on her third orgasm.

I knew he knew how to eat some pussy. Wonder what his dick game is like. Get it together Taylor. No fucking yet you gotta stay in control. Taylor's thoughts were interrupted by her brewing orgasm. "Shit," she exclaimed as she came.

Alex rubbed her clit with his finger as he slurped up all of her juices, not leaving a drop. He smiled at the look of pleasure on Taylor's face. He stood up and grabbed her hand. He placed it on the bulge in his pants.

"You taste even better than I imagined. He wants to play, but I'm going to be a gentleman. Unless you don't want me too."

Hell no I don't want you to be. Got damn he holding. I know that shit's good. Taylor took a deep breath before she responded.

"I'll take the gentleman for now." She smiled and then added playfully, "At least until our third date."

"Shit we can plan date three now!"

She laughed and kissed him. Alex kneeled down and grabbed her jeans and pulled them up.

"I'm sorry about your panties. I'll make sure you get some new ones."

Taylor really wasn't thinking about panties. The money he was dropping was enough to buy a hundred pair of panties.

They ordered Chinese food and watched *Law Abiding Citizen;* after which Taylor called the car service to pick her up. Alex offered to take her home, but of course per Sylvia's guidance that was a big no-no. She politely declined his offer and waited for the car.

Once Taylor got home she fixed herself a glass of wine and ran a bath. *Perfect way to end a perfect night,* she thought as she reminisced on the night. Taylor couldn't wait to see what Alex had in stored for date three.

Chapter 3

"I'll show her. Talking about I don't have what it takes to run the business. Bitch. All I asked was for you to teach me, fuck show me. Now I'll teach myself and build bigger than you," Sade said pacing in her apartment.

Sylvia implied to Sade that at forty-five she was getting too old to run the business and was contemplating an apprentice. Sylvia laughed at Sade when she said she'd like to be that person.

"Silly girl. You are not "Misses" material. You are a pretty girl with a beautiful body. Use that."

Sade just stood there in shock that Sylvia had told her that she was only beauty and no brains. Sylvia did not get the hint from Sade's silence and continued.

"You're not a Taylor. Now she's beautiful and smart. She's just started and has shown great potential."

Taylor? Wow. Sade remained silent and left Sylvia's home. She'd been compared to Taylor damn near her whole life and Sade hated that.

****

Taylor had been in the business for almost a year when she experienced her first glimpse of the ugliness that came with being an escort. She was on a date with the owner of several local storage container companies; Joseph Mouzan. "Joey" as he told her to call him was a real sleaze ball. Unlike her other "Benjamins" (Taylor's nickname for the men to remind her it was all about the Benjamins. Money over emotions.) he didn't want companionship; he flat out wanted to fuck. Joseph exploited women on a regular.

Outside of her sugar daddy Alex, Taylor had only slept with two other Benjamins over the course of the year; each with a hefty price tag. Taylor had no desire to sleep with Joseph. Besides the fact that she had no attraction to the oily haired grungy looking man, he had her meet him in a hotel room.

Joseph's intent was evident from the door. Though it was a nice hotel her "hell no" buzzer went off once she got to the room. Taylor ignored the warnings though and attempted to get through the date.

Joseph greeted Taylor with a cheesy grin. There was a table set for two with room service trays and two glasses of wine; which Taylor didn't like one bit. One thing her late fiancé taught her was to never except drinks if she didn't see it delivered. He owned a club so he had stories for days about people getting drugs dropped in their drinks. She adapted that philosophy with food as well. With her extracurricular activities she could never be too careful.

"Have a seat beautiful. I'm Joey, and you are?"

"Nice to meet you Joey. I'm Virtue."

"Virtue? That's different."

"Growing up I was told that I was different; in a good way of course," she said throwing a soft smile his way.

"Well, I've ordered dinner for us." He took the lids off the covered trays. "We have salmon, wild rice, and broccoli. I hope you like salmon."

She loved salmon actually, but she was not going to eat it. *Damn it smells good.*

"I'm so sorry, I'm allergic to fish. Can I order something else?"

His look told Taylor that he did not like that. "Sure," he said through a forced smile. "You're not allergic to Merlot are you?" he asked sarcastically.

"No I'm not, but sorry I don't drink alcohol."

Another lie. That was true prior to Will's murder. Now a glass (or two) of wine was usually how she ended her nights.

"Well I be damn. Sylvia sent me a goodie two shoes whore this time," he slurred.

"Excuse me?"

"You heard me. I didn't stutter you whore bitch."

It took everything in her power not to flip all the way out. *Breathe. Don't go hood on this ignorant ass motherfucker.* Taylor grabbed her purse.

"Excuse me sir but this evening is over," she said as she stood up.

Joseph got right up on her.

"It's over when I say it's over. I paid for your time. So I'll tell you what's going to happen and how it's going to happen. So take your ass over to that bed so I can throw you this bone."

"No I will not, and I advise you to get your nasty ass out of my face."

Joseph drew back and slapped Taylor.

"Shut up you black slut bitch," he snarled.

Taylor stood in shock for half a second before she pulled her stun gun from her purse and rammed it into Joseph's groin area. He let out a high pitched scream as he fell to the ground.

"You bitch as motherfucker," Taylor yelled as she sent more shock waves to his balls. She got madder as she felt the intensified sting on her face. "You fucking hit me! In my fucking face! I'ma show you that this black slut bitch ain't the one to be fucked with," she said as she moved the stun gun to his asshole. "Take that you pussy."

Joseph was in tears by the time Taylor eased up off the stun gun. She left him on the floor and went downstairs to her waiting car...mad then a motherfucker.

****

Sade hardly worked at the salon any more. Her schedule was packed with escort appointments. Not only was she doing the dates that Sylvia set, she was also moonlighting with her own dates.

Sade started calling past dates to "chit chat". Several took the bait and she went on these spur of the moment dates that resulted in instant cash in her hands. She also got referrals from the guys she had closer relationships with.

The night of Taylor's incident Sade was on a date with Albert Castello. She called him her "Italian Stallion"; he satisfied her all around.

The Italian New York native lived in Savannah, Georgia but frequently visited Atlanta for business.

Albert owned a car dealership in Savannah but Sade suspected he was into pushing cocaine as well. She didn't care though; money was money. Sade felt like how he got his money was his wife's issue and not hers.

Albert took Sade to one of the most upscale restaurants in Atlanta, *Baccanalia*, for dinner. They were at dinner when Taylor called the first time. Sade looked down at her phone and silenced it. *Probably want to complain about her date. I don't have time for her tonight. I'll call her in the morning.*

Albert spared no expense when it came to spending time with Sade. Sade set her sights on him early. She gave him the best head he'd ever had as a sample of her abilities. He quickly dropped a thousand dollars in her lap for her goodies. She fucked his brains out like her life depended on it. The rest was history; expensive dates, rent payments, gifts, and loyalty. Albert never hired anyone else. Sade told him that his wife would be the only woman she'd share him with. Up until that point their arrangement was working out great.

"Baby, I'm ready to get to your room so you can show me how much you missed me," Sade said during dessert.

Albert smiled and got the waiter's attention.

"Can we get the check please?" he said to the young man.

Taylor called Sade two more times that night, but Sade was in Albert's hotel room, legs up getting dicked down by her Italian Stallion.

****

"Fuck. Sade, where the hell are you at?" Taylor said after the third unanswered call. *Probably somewhere fucking.*

Taylor was still steaming from her date. She went home, got herself some wine, and put ice on her face. The wine really calmed her because she got pissed off every time she thought about the night. Taylor knew she had to talk to Sylvia, but she'd do that the next day.

Taylor showered and got in bed. She calmed her nerves by ending her night with her "Mr. Reliable". She kept him close in the top drawer of her night stand. Taylor massaged her vagina walls with the six inch vibrator until the emotions of the night were replaced with the feeling of ecstasy. She had a peaceful night's sleep.

Chapter 4

Taylor didn't let the incident with Joseph break her; it actually made her more focused. She'd spoken to Sylvia who attempted to be empathetic, but Taylor saw straight through her act. Sylvia was about her money. She'd mentioned the fact that she refunded Joseph his money several times but never once said she would not take his business again.

Taylor knew right then that Sylvia did not have her back. She was glad that Alex had purchased her the stun gun for protection. Since that date with Joseph, Taylor never went on any job unprotected.

Taylor and Sade hardly spoke anymore. Taylor knew she was up to something but she could never catch up with her to find out what. She didn't worry too much. Though Sade was quite impulsive, she knew how to take care of herself. Taylor knew they'd catch up with one another in due time; they never went too long without talking.

****

Taylor pulled her Honda into the parking lot of Brown & Brown Law associates. Her black and white Jimmy Choo pumps hit the pavement and exposed her leg up to her black knee length skirt.

"Damn," Rick, one of the paralegals at Brown & Brown said.

Rick had been crushing on Taylor ever since he started.

"Good morning Rick. It's too early for me to be dealing with your mess."

"I can't help it Taylor. You know you're finer than a motherfucker. I don't know why you won't give me the time of day."

"First off, we work together. I keep my business and personal life very separate. Second, I'm good on that relationship stuff."

He rushed and opened the door for her as they approached the building.

"Alright now. Just keep me in mind if anything changes," he said with a smile.

Taylor returned the smile and said, "I will."

Rick was fine. He had all the qualities that turned Taylor on; tall, mocha brown skin, broad shoulders, chiseled abs, and gorgeous teeth. Unfortunately for him Taylor wasn't about nothing but dollars.

Taylor walked down the hall to her office. She turned back to see Rick watching her ass as she walked. She shook her head and continued on her way.

Taylor was greeted by her assistant Megan when she entered the office, "Good morning Ms. Jones."

"Good morning Megan. Anything hot come up this morning?"

"Yes ma'am. The budget meeting was moved from three to eleven in the conference room with a catered lunch afterwards in the meeting room."

"Okay. Great. Anything else?"

"No ma'am. Would you like me to fix your coffee?"

"Megan you're the best. Thank you."

"No problem Ms. Jones," Megan said grinning from ear to ear. She knew how to keep Taylor happy.

Taylor checked her emails and went through the firm's accounts receivable and payable to ensure her information was accurate for her meeting.

Taylor shined during the budget meeting as usual. The partners were very happy with her performance because she was great at what she did. After the meeting Taylor took her things to her office and then moved toward the meeting room with added confidence. Taylor walked into the meeting room and the partners were huddled in the corner.

She heard Alfred, the senior partner say, "Let me introduce you to our head of accounting Taylor," to a gentleman as she walked to them.

The gentleman turned around and Taylor slowed her steps; it was Alex. Both were shocked to see the other.

Ain't no way. Breathe, hold it together.

"Taylor this is my brother Alex. Alex this is Taylor. Don't let her innocent look fool you because she's a corporate pit bull."

Taylor smiled.

"Hello Alex. Nice to meet you," she said in hopes of Alex going along and not blowing up her spot.

Alex grabbed her hand and kissed it, "Nice to meet you as well. Taylor it is?"

"Yes, it is."

Taylor's mind raced as Alfred proudly bragged on his younger brother's success. She concentrated on maintaining a pleasant smile and not showcasing her internal turmoil. Taylor was relieved when they announced that lunch was served. She excused herself from the conversation.

Taylor stepped out into the hallway to catch her breath. She'd been so careful to keep her secret life a secret for over a year and did not want to have it revealed. It was imperative that she kept Taylor's and Virtue's lives separate.

Fuck! Taylor's melt down was interrupted by Megan.

"Ms. Jones are you alright? You look flustered. Do you want me to get you some water?"

"Thank you Megan, but I'll be alright. I got a little nauseous. I think someone's cologne didn't agree with me."

"I know the feeling. That happens to me sometimes."

Taylor forced a smile.

"Are you ready for lunch?"

"Yes ma'am. I'm starving."

"Me too."

Taylor got through the luncheon and mentally prepared for the conversation she knew her and Alex were going to have.

****

Alex and Alfred were in Alfred's office.

"Bro you alright? You've been quiet since the luncheon."

"I'm good."

"Shitting me. What's up?"

"Remember the chick I was telling you I'd been hanging out with?"

"The escort chick?"

"Yeah Virtue. Well..."

"Well what?"

"Taylor is Virtue."

"Get the fuck out of here. Nah, you got to be shitting me. Where's the cameras? She is one of the most put together women I know. She doesn't even give any of these dudes here a second glance. I don't believe that shit."

"For real. I told you she wasn't like any normal escort. I knew she was different."

"Shit," Alfred said in a defeated tone. "I'm gonna have to let her go."

"Nah, man. I'm coming to you as my brother not a lawyer at Brown & Brown."

"But if the other partners find out-"

"They won't. Hell you wouldn't have found out if I didn't stop by here to take you to lunch. She'd hid it this long and obviously it hadn't affected her work. Promise me you won't let her go bro."

"Okay. But if shit hits the fan I'm going to deny my knowledge of any of this and she's gone."

"Alright."

"Well, you've confirmed my guess."

"What guess?"

"That she had that fire pussy, because I know you've dropped some loot on her. I might have to test that water."

"Fuck no you don't. Shit, there's plenty more water you can test."

"I was just fucking with you. I wouldn't do that to you. You all in love and shit."

"Whatever man. What's up with the golf though? You gonna meet me at the club?"

"Yeah. Let me handle a few things here. Meet you at three."

"Cool."

"See you then."

"See ya."

Alex left and immediately called Taylor.

****

Taylor had just finished her weekly balance sheet when Alex called her Virtue cell phone.

"Hello."

"Hello, Virtue or should I say Taylor?"

"Virtue."

"Okay. Needless to say I was quite surprised to see you today. Happy but surprised. We've been spending a lot of time together and you hadn't even told me your real name."

"Actually Virtue is my middle name. I keep my personal life separate. I am a professional. What I'm doing is frowned upon in the cooperate world and I enjoy my job."

"Well, you don't have to worry about that. My brother knows

how I feel about you."

How you feel about me?

"You told Mr. Brown?"

"Yes."

"Damn it Alex!"

"Calm down baby. It's okay. He's my brother and he wouldn't do that to me. I love you too much to see you hurt. So no worries."

Love me too much? Taylor decided to not pry into that statement.

"I hope you're right Alex. If not you better be ready to take care of me; mortgage, car note, clothes, food, the whole nine."

"I got you babe," he said with a chuckle.

"I ain't playing. So Mr. Brown is your blood brother?"

"Yes. My half brother; we have different dads. My last name is Grimes after my father. Brown was my mother's maiden name."

"Cool. So are we still on for tonight?"

"Of course. I'm going to play golf at three, but I'll be done by six. So I'm thinking about seven-thirty or eight o'clock? We can grab a bite and then you can be my dessert."

"Sounds good."

"Great come by the house and we can go from there."

"Okay. See you there. Have fun at the course."

"Thanks baby."

Taylor was uneasy about him informing his brother of her side hustle, but she could only hope for the best. Unfortunately the "best" did not happen. For months Alfred would send subliminal messages

Taylor's way. She ignored him and went about her daily routine.

One day Taylor was in the copy room copying some documents. Usually she would have sent Megan but it was personal documents for her money market account. Alfred entered the copy room and got up on Taylor. He invaded her personal space so quickly that it startled her and she jumped.

"What are you jumpy for Taylor? You should be used to this type of closeness in your line of work."

"No, I'm not used to this type of closeness as an accountant. Your accountant I must add so if you don't mind I need you to back away from me. I'd hate for an issue of sexual harassment to arise."

"Are you threatening me?" he said as he laughed. Not just any laugh but a gut buster type laugh.

Taylor watched as he had a good laugh at her expense.

"Did I say something funny?"

He contained his laugh and said, "Yes. As a matter a fact you did. You here soliciting sex in your free time, which is against our ethics and morals clause I must add, and you want to get all 'an issue of sexual harassment' with me. Hilarious. I got something for your sexual harassment issue. The fact that you're lucky I don't bend you over that copy machine and fuck the shit out of you. How about that? As a matter a fact I foresee us having a rendezvous that involves me fucking the shit out of you. That is if you enjoy working here as much as you claim you do."

No this motherfucker ain't threatening me. I got something for that ass. I'll let him think he won this one.

"Wow. I thought you were better than this, but I love my job. One time, that is it and you cannot tell your brother," she pleaded.

"Okay. I like this submissive side of you; got my dick hard. Tomorrow night. I'll tell you where to meet me around seven."

"Okay. Now get out of my way."

He smiled and moved aside.

Dick head.

Taylor had a plan and she needed her girl's help. She picked up her phone and called Sade.

"Glad you answered. I need a huge favor. I'll stop by when I get off to fill you in."

"Okay."

Let the games begin.

Chapter 5

Taylor shot Alfred a wink the morning after their sexual rendezvous. She smiled as she went to her office because she had the upper hand. Alfred had the intent of fucking the shit out of Taylor but he was the one that got fucked.

Taylor and Sade met him at a Holiday Inn in Covington, Georgia. She assumed he choose the out skirts of Atlanta because he didn't want to run into any one that he knew; seeing as he was married. Alfred was both surprised and excited when he saw Sade with Taylor.

"Damn a two for one. I'm a lucky man."

Taylor smiled, "Yes. This is my friend Shay. I want to ensure you're satisfied enough to stand by your word. I don't want to lose my job, so let's do this."

"Glad you decided to see things my way. I always knew you were a smart girl. So…"

His words trailed off when Sade dropped the trench coat she was wearing. He did everything but drool seeing Sade standing there in a leather bustier, hot pants, and thigh high boots. Sade was rocking the outfit. When Taylor saw Sade's outfit she'd told her that she'd want to fuck if she went that way. Sade laughed but Taylor was serious.

"Damn," Alfred said.

"You like daddy?" Sade asked as she bent over to give him the full view of her ass.

Alfred was speechless. He nodded his head with a foolish grin on his face. Taylor smiled, *this shit is gonna be easier than I thought with his desperate ass. Wife probably ain't giving his ass any anyway.*

While Sade flirted with Alfred, Taylor opened up her bag of tricks. Her eyes focused on a pair of handcuffs, a blindfold, a camera, and a strap on. Sade swayed Alfred to the bed as Taylor dropped her trench coat and exposed her leather cat suit.

"It's all about you daddy. You gonna play nice? I need you to be a good boy and do everything that I say," Sade said emphasizing on everything.

Sade moved close to his ear.

"This will be a night to remember. I promise," she said before she licked his earlobe.

Sade had him eating out of her hands. Alfred nodded his head like he was in a trance as Sade kissed him softly on his lips. Sade looked over at Taylor who smiled and gave a slow head nod.

Let the fun begin.

"You ready for the best time of your life?" Taylor asked Alfred.

"Hell yeah," Alfred said anxiously.

"Good. Stand up," Taylor said giving him a peck on the lips.

Alfred stood up and Taylor unbuttoned his shirt as Sade undid his pants. They both kissed and caressed his body as they undressed him; Taylor high and Sade low until he stood naked. *He's working with a little something,* Taylor thought as she looked down. *Too bad he had to be such a dick. His bad.*

Taylor heard Alfred moan. Sade had started sucking his semi erect penis so Taylor undressed and went to her bag of goodies. Sade sat Alfred down on the bed as Taylor grabbed the blindfold and the stimulating oil. Alfred attempted to object when Taylor went to place the blindfold on him.

"Shhhh," she said placing her finger to his lips.

"You agreed to play nice. Remember? You don't need to see. All you need to do is feel. Start with these," Taylor said as she placed his hands on her perky breast. He felt on them like a teenage boy who got his first feel.

"Tonight I want you to be sexually free. Any and everything goes tonight so no more resistance."

Between Taylor's breast and the head Sade gave Alfred, it was enough for him to relax as Taylor blindfolded him. Taylor pushed him back on the bed, kissed his midsection, moved to his chest and nipples, kissed his lips, and ended her journey by sitting on his face.

Taylor rode Alfred's face while Sade continued to suck his dick. Sade grabbed the stimulating oil and squeezed it on Alfred's balls. She tickled his dick with her tongue as she massaged his balls. Sade moved down and massaged his asshole.

Alfred flinched when Sade touched his hole so she circled his balls with her tongue. Once Alfred relaxed, she played around the area again. This time sticking her thumb in the hole as she deep throated his dick. The sensation immobilized him, but Taylor didn't give him a pass on his eating. She gyrated back and forth on his tongue until she came on his face. Taylor moaned as she released her sweetness. Then she turned around, spread her ass cheeks, and sat back on his face. Alfred grabbed her ass and went to town. *Well alright now Mr. Brown,* she thought as she grinded on him. Taylor caught Sade's eye as Alfred was eating her ass. Taylor knew it was time to move to phase two of the foreplay.

Taylor got up and took over the dick sucking while Sade went and got undressed. Sade took off everything except for her boots.

She moved back to the bed and whispered, "Are you ready for me daddy?" into Alfred's ear.

"Yes. Bring that sexy ass here."

Sade straddled Alfred backwards giving it to him in the sixty nine position. She licked and nibbled at his mid section, before she took over the dick sucking from Taylor who moved to his balls.

Alfred moaned from the sensation both of their mouths brought. Taylor stuck her finger into his ass as Sade continued sucking his balls. He tensed at first until Sade tickled his head with her tongue.

Taylor handed Sade a condom. She used her mouth to roll it on his shaft. Alfred, who was still blindfolded, laid there anticipating her wetness.

"You ready for me daddy?" Sade asked as she moved from his face.

"Hell yeah."

"You sure you're ready for this hot wet pussy?"

"Fuck yeah."

"Show me then," she said as she mounted him.

"Damn," he blurted out when Sade sat on him.

"Is that shit good to you daddy?"

"Oh yeah."

"Good. Now grab my ass and throw that shit back at me."

Sade let out shrills of pleasure as he followed her instruction. All the while Taylor grabbed what she needed from the bag. Sade got a good nut and told Alfred to taste it.

Alfred took the blindfold off and flipped Sade over. She played with her titties as Alfred buried his face in her pussy. He was so focused on Sade that he was oblivious to what Taylor was doing. She'd donned the strap on and had the camera in her hand.

Taylor caressed and kissed Alfred's back as she dripped more stimulating oil down his butt. She simultaneously played with his balls and ass hole.

"You ready to get nasty daddy?" Sade asked.

He nodded his head yes.

"You ready for the best nut you'd ever had."

Another head nod.

"Trust me okay."

"Okay."

With that Taylor moved her finger and put the head of the strap on in his ass."

"What the-"

"No no. Trust me," Sade said as she moved over to the side and began jacking him off.

Alfred relaxed and Taylor entered him deeper with slow thrust until he took all seven inches of Taylor's strapped on dick. She continued with slow thrust until he was about to cum, then she and Sade both sped up their motion. Alfred let out an extended groan as his cum shot into the condom.

"Fuck..."

"Told you to trust me. That shit was good huh?"

"Shit yeah."

Sade shoved her tongue down Alfred's throat. She was so turned on by the whole scene that she had nut dripping down her thighs. She got Alfred back right so he could scratch her itch.

Taylor went into the bathroom. She checked the camera to ensure the footage was captured; she caught her putting on the strap on, Alfred eating Sade's pussy, and the entire act of her fucking him. Ultimately a video that no man, especially one married with children, would want anyone to see. Taylor was sure not to get her or Sade's face in the video.

Checkmate bitch, she thought with a smile.

Taylor took a quick shower while Alfred beat Sade down in the bedroom. She was not only happy that Sade agreed to help her (though her debt eventually landed her in that tub), but also that she was having some enjoyable sex. Taylor was glad she got through the evening without him sticking his dick in her.

Can't stand that motherfucker.

Taylor and Sade left Alfred in the hotel room sprawled out on the bed. When she got home she uploaded the video to her computer, saved a copy, and sent it to Alfred with a friendly fuck you email. She slept like a boss that night.

Chapter 6

"So what you think about my proposal Al?"

Albert sat contemplating what Sade had asked him.

"Come on baby. I can't do it without you. Let's make this money together."

"Honey, I sell cars-."

"That's all?" Sade cut in with, looking at him sideways.

"Well, I don't sell ass. That's for damn sure. I won't know the first thing to do sweets."

"But I do. That's the beauty of it babes."

"What about Sylvia?"

"Man fuck Sylvia!"

Albert looked at Sade crazy. He was not used to Sade being loud.

"I'm just saying. We can do this. She doesn't even have to know."

"I hear you Shay baby, but Sylvia is cut throat when it comes to business. She's old school ruthless."

"I know but I work close enough to her to make sure we do it right. Just trust me. Let's make this money," she said coaxing him with soft kisses.

"You know that shit drives me crazy."

"Well, say yes so you can give me some good loving baby."

Sade kissed all around his neck and ran her fingers through his hair.

"Say yes baby. Say yes."

Weak from Sade's sexual aura he agreed.

"Thank you daddy," she said before she unzipped his pants and placed his manhood in her mouth.

****

Taylor was out on a date with one of Atlanta's local celebrities, Stacey Hendricks. Stacey was a music producer. He was a god on Atlanta's underground rap scene. His secretary hired Taylor to accompany Stacey to a launch party for one of his artist. From what Stacey told Taylor they didn't want a thirsty groupie chick on his arm so there she was. Taylor thought there might have been another reason she was there. Since the Donte situation she began picking up on what she thought to be down low behavior. Stacey was a little suspect to her. Either way, Taylor didn't care because money was money.

It had been a while since she'd been to a club so it was different; especially since she wasn't with her girls Chyna and Sade. Stacey was good company and Taylor enjoyed herself. She had been to some nice events on her dates but Club Met was the best. They sat in VIP, but it was unlike any other VIP Taylor had ever been in before. It was a very upscale club. The furniture was plush and there was expensive wine, champagne, and hor d'oeuvres being passed around.

Taylor's clutch began to vibrate as she sat with Stacey. She grabbed the phone out of her purse and saw that it was Alex. She quickly rejected the call.

Things had not been the same between Taylor and Alex since her episode with Alfred. She didn't know if it was that part of her felt guilty or if it was the fact that she hated his brother just that much. Either way she'd distanced herself from him. It did not stop his attempts though.

Taylor placed the phone back into her purse and began grooving to the music. Stacey wasn't the dancing type so she contained her dancing to her chair; ensuring she kept it sexy.

By the end of the night Taylor was in lots of pictures and all over Twitter and Facebook. She felt like a celebrity for the night.

"Hey Virtue me and the crew are having an after party by my crib. You wanna come?"

Taylor looked at her watch and saw it was two in the morning. She had to be at work the next morning but was like what the hell.

"Sure."

"Cool. I'm bout ready to get out of here."

"Cool."

Taylor thought about Sade and how much she'd enjoy the whole scene.

"Stacey, would you mind if I invite my girl?"

"Is she as fine as you?"

"Actually she is."

"Cool with me. The more fine honeys the better. The address is 1297 South Boulevard."

"Okay. I'm going to go to the restroom and call her. I'll be right back."

Taylor checked her face as Sade's phone rang. If it was anyone else, she would not dare call them at two in the morning, but Sade was a night owl.

"Hello. You alright Tay?"

"Yeah I'm good. What you doing?"

"Smoking a blunt and cooling out."

"Guess who I'm with."

"Who?"

"Stacey Hendricks."

"Who?"

"The music producer that produced Lil' Cash and D Money's shit."

"Ohhhh shit. That's what's up."

"We at Club Met right now. He had a launch party for a new cat's album. Anyways, they're having an after party at his house. I asked him if I could invite you. So get your ass up and get cute. I'll text you the address."

"Shiiiit, bout to get up now. Good looking out Tay."

"That's how we do. Hit me up when you on your way."

"Okay."

Taylor texted Sade the address and then applied some fresh lip gloss to her lips. She went back out to the VIP section to Stacey.

"Ready to go sexy?" he asked when she got back.

"I'm ready if you are."

Stacey gave Taylor his arm and they made their way through the club. Taylor was getting comfortable in Stacey's car when she spotted a silver Corvette like Alex's. Alex was not a clubber so she didn't even think twice that it could be him. However, she was wrong. Alex had followed her and Stacey to the club that night. He got a table in a corner that gave him a clear view of Taylor and her every move.

****

Alex had not been happy about Taylor not spending that much time with him. He thought they had a good thing going on and couldn't understand why things had changed.

Unknowingly to Taylor, Alex had followed her quite option. He watched her run, watched her on dates, and watched her from outside of her home. He'd developed an obsession with Taylor that he could not shake. Watching her made him feel close to her.

Alex sat in the shadows and watched as Taylor danced and had a good time. He hated that he wasn't the one putting a smile on her face. Was his brother right and he'd fallen in love with her? He didn't know what he was feeling but he knew he felt lost without her.

Alex got angry when Taylor grabbed Stacey's arm and left the club. *I bet she's going to go fuck him. I can't let her do that. I've invested too much time, attention, and money into her. I have to put a stop to her hoe days,* he thought as his nostrils flared.

****

Stacey's party was off the hook. Taylor thought it was going to be an after party with maybe five or six of Stacey's friends, but there ended up being at least fifty people there. Taylor wasn't down for some of the activities such as weed smoking and pill popping, but she still had a great time.

Sade arrived about forty five minutes after they got to the house.

"Girl it's thick in here. Glad I wore my fuck me pumps," Sade said with a laugh.

"You rocking them too girl!"

"Thank you, thank you very much," she replied showcasing her shoes.

They both laughed and moved about the party. It didn't take Sade long to set her sights on Stacey's younger brother Quincy. Quincy was a fine caramel man; six-four, athletic build, pretty eyes, great smile, and dimples.

Taylor was surprised to see Sade hugged up in the corner with him because he was a little cleaner cut than Sade liked them. She usually didn't give guys like Quincy the time of day. *Must be the dollar signs,* Taylor thought before she was tapped on the shoulder.

She turned around, "Alex? What are you doing here?"

"What I'm not doing is drinking myself crazy, doing drugs, or ducking off into rooms to have sexual orgies like the rest of these clowns. What are you doing here Taylor? I thought you were a smart girl. This..." he said pointing around the room, "Is not smart. Every other night after your dates you go home and have some wine, but tonight you decided to come to this clown's house."

"What the fuck? Wait. Wait a minute. Have you been following me?"

"It's not like that," Alex started before Taylor interjected.

"It's not like what? That you are fucking following me. Excuse me, stalking me."

"Taylor I love you and I worry about you. That's all," he said as he reached for her hand.

"No. Stay the fuck away from me. If I see you around my house you better be ready to catch a bullet."

Taylor walked off and went over to Sade and Quincy.

She grabbed Sade's arm and said, "Shay I need you to take me home."

"But Tay me and Q are just getting acquainted. Is everything okay?"

"Alex is here and I just found out he's been following me. I need to get out of here. I'm going to call the car service."

"Damn shorty that's fucked up," Quincy added.

Taylor gave him the "mind your fucking business" look. He caught the hint and didn't say anything else.

"Take my car Tay. I'm sure Q wouldn't mind taking me home. Would you cutie?"

"I got you ma."

Sade gave Taylor her keys.

"Are you sure?" Taylor asked.

"Yeah, I'm good. Call me when you get home. I got my piece in my spot in the car if you need it."

"Thanks Shay," Taylor said and gave Sade a hug.

Taylor got into Sade's Mustang. She locked the door and grabbed the gun from the secret compartment under the floor board. The whole situation shook her but she felt better once she sat the gun on the seat beside her.

Taylor's mind raced the entire drive home. She'd been so worried about keeping her secret life a secret that she'd become slack. She knew the situation could have been a lot worst and hoped it didn't get there.

Taylor texted Sade when she got home. She poured her normal glass of unwinding wine. The difference that night was she accompanied her wine with a hand gun with one in the chamber.

Chapter 7

Taylor did not have any problems out of Alex after the night of Stacey's party. He'd made attempts to explain himself, but quickly gave up when Taylor ignored those attempts. To her knowledge he had not been lurking around; which she was happy about.

Taylor was relieved to be done with the shenanigans of Alex and his brother; both turned out being a pain in her ass. She didn't worry about Alfred though, because she still had his balls in a sling with the video.

"Ms. Jones, I'm about to go to lunch. I'm going to the Starbucks around the corner. Would you like to go with or want me to bring you something back?" Megan said to Taylor.

"I'm good Megan. Thanks for asking."

"Are you sure? You look like you can go for an iced coffee. It's a nice day out. You need to get out of this office," Megan said in a coaxing tone.

"Okay... Let me get my purse."

The Starbucks was only a block away so the ladies decided to walk. *Damn, these are thousand dollar shoes. Hope I don't scuff them,* Taylor thought as they walked down the sidewalk.

"It's a nice day," Megan said smiling.

Taylor enjoyed being around Megan because she had a bubbly personality. Between her personality and her work ethic Taylor loved having Megan as an assistant.

"Yes it is. Thanks for pulling me out of the office."

The ladies reached the Starbucks that was packed with the professionals that worked in the area. After a lengthy wait Taylor and Megan were able to order. She'd just paid for her and Megan's ice coffee and Panini sandwiches when she ran into a gentleman as she turned from the counter.

"Oh, excuse me. My apologies."

"No problem," the man said.

He towered over Taylor at six feet three, evenly tanned skin, a gorgeous smile, and amazing sky blue eyes.

"You can bump into me anytime beautiful," he said shooting her his perfect smile.

I know this white boy is not flirting with me, she thought.

"I'm Philip by the way and you are?" he said extending his hand.

"Taylor," she said reaching to shake his hand.

"Nice to meet you."

"Yes. Well my apologies again for bumping into you. You have a nice day."

Taylor walked off to her table leaving Philip speechless. Though

Taylor caught Philip watching her a few times as she ate her sandwich and drunk her iced coffee, she acted as if he was invisible. She did not entertain his flirting because he was not her type. Not only had she never dated outside of her race, but he was dirty. Philip was a construction worker who was working on the building next door to the Starbucks.

Taylor remained engaged in Megan's conversation. Though Megan was a good girl she stayed having man problems. That along with her lack of extra money made her a great candidate for escorting. *Too bad I don't mix my day and night world cause I'd put her on.* Taylor gave Megan the "it'll all work out" speech and they left and went back to their office. Taylor left not giving Philip another thought.

****

Sade was all smiles as she made her way to the bank. Business was booming from her side deals. She'd been careful to not let Sylvia get wind of her extra dealings. Once she'd gotten Albert to agree to back her, she intended to get some girls to work for her. Sade knew she needed to be very selective on whom and it could not be any of the girls that worked for Sylvia. Truth be told she didn't trust none of those hoes other than Taylor. With that being true, she hadn't even told Taylor about what she was doing. Sade wanted to save herself the motherly lecture she knew Taylor would give her.

Sade's cell phone rang as she sat in the bank's parking lot. It was Quincy; they'd hooked up occasionally since the party at Stacey's. Sade wasn't the one for shit like relationships and love, but after he fucked the shit out of her that night she made a decision to keep him around.

"Hey sweets," she said as she answered the phone.

"Hey baby girl. What you up to?"

"Just doing some running around. What's up with you?"

"Ain't shit. Just thinking about you sitting that fat pussy on my face."

Hell yeah!

"Oh yeah?"

"Yeah and I'm thinking about how that ass claps when I'm deep in that pussy."

"Hmmmm. So what do you propose we do about these vivid images that you're thinking of?"

"I propose that you bring that ass over here so I can make you feel good."

"Just like that?"

"Yep exactly like that. Don't you like the way I make that pussy cum?"

Fuck yeah!

"You do aight."

"Aight? Bet. You'll pay for that later. By the time I'm done with you I want that pussy to be calling my name. So bring your fine ass over here. I'll be waiting," he said and hung up.

Sade loved that he was so demanding and didn't take no shit from her. She needed a strong man to put her in her place. Sade made her bank deposit and went to Quincy's; ready to be punished for her slick mouth.

****

Taylor had been thinking about Will a lot. He'd visited her several times in her dreams. The dreams always ended with him kissing her and telling her he was still watching over her.

Taylor decided to take a day to herself; no friends, no Benjamins, and no Sylvia. Taylor had wanted to go to the aquarium since she'd moved to Atlanta, so she got cute in a long sundress, sandals, light make up, and went.

Taylor was standing in front of the shark tank when she was tapped on the shoulder. Startled she turned around.

"I'm sorry to startle you. I just wanted to say hello."

Taylor was confused. The gentleman looked familiar but she could not place him.

"I'm sorry. Do I know you?"

"So you bump into a guy and forget all about him? I'm Philip. We met at Starbucks last week."

"Oh yes. You look different outside of your work clothes."

Different equated to fine. He was clean shaven and dressed in a polo shirt, khaki shorts (which showcased some amazing tattoo work), and Sperrys. Taylor felt he pulled off the preppy look really well.

"Yes, soap and water works miracles. Dust and dirt usually aren't part of my normal attire," he said with a chuckle. "You are looking beautiful as usual."

"Thank you," she said blushing.

That slight moment of vulnerability was snatched away when a little boy ran up and grabbed Philip's hand.

"I want to go see the dolphins. Come on. Come on. You said give you one minute and it's been lots."

Taylor stood stunned. The young boy appeared to be about five.

Damn, he's a fine ass white boy but I do not do any baby mama drama. No way.

"Billy, don't you see me talking to this pretty lady? What should you have done?"

"Said excuse me. Sorry Uncle Philip. I just got so excited."

Uncle, she thought with a smile on her face.

"It's okay. This is Ms. Taylor. Tell her hello."

"Hello," he said reaching for her hand.

"Hi," Taylor said as he shook her hand.

"Taylor I would love to talk to you more. If you're here alone, maybe you'd like to go see the dolphins with us."

She was a sucker for a great smile and Philip had one.

What the hell?

"Sure."

"Great."

Taylor, Philip, and Billy moved through the entire aquarium with lots of smiles and laughs. Afterwards they went and got some pizza. Taylor really enjoyed Philip's company and they exchanged numbers before they left the pizza joint. She replayed the day and the unsuspected connection on her drive home. It was both weird and nice at the same time.

Chapter 8

Taylor was lounging on her couch when her door bell rang. *Who the hell is that?* "Who is it?" she yelled from the couch as she got up.

"It's Shay."

Taylor opened the door.

"Hey girl. What you doing over this way?"

"Don't hey girl me. I came to check on you since your ass been up under a rock for the past month."

"Ah stop it."

"No I'm not. What's been up? We ain't been talking and you've been doing less and less jobs. Your ass done fucked around and fell in love or some shit?"

"Well..."

"Oh hell," Sade said as she took a seat on the couch. "Spill it."

"I wouldn't say I'm in love, but Philip and I have been spending a lot of time together."

"The white boy?"

"Yes," Taylor said with a giggle.

"Hey we all can use some cream in our coffee cause my sugar Al be loading my cup."

"You're silly," Taylor said laughing.

"Call it what you want but that shit is good."

"I don't know about that...yet."

"What!?! Y'all been kicking it for what about three or four months now and you ain't test the water?"

"Nope. We do a lot of snuggling and what not but no sex yet."

"That dude's gay!"

"No he's not."

Taylor paused thinking about Donte and then added, "I hope not anyways. He says he wants our first time to be special and not rushed."

"Yeah okay. I'll take gay for a thousand Alex. So you're not in love and you're not getting dicked down so why the hell have you been missing? Don't fuck up your money because of a possibility. Money over emotions. Remember?"

"I'm not. Plus I'm not hurting for money. I've been letting my money work for me in the stock market and let me say my portfolio is looking very nice."

"Well alright Ms. Money Bags, but a bitch like me can always use more money."

"Stick with me and continue doing what I tell you to and you will be Ms. Money Bags too."

"Okay. Well I'm glad to see you're alright and not in a ditch somewhere. I'm about to go get my hair done. I'll holla at you later."

"Okay. Thanks for stopping by."

They hugged and Sade left.

Taylor went back to the couch. Her phone went off as she laid there. When she looked down it was a message from Philip. *"I want tonight to be that special night. Pick you up at seven."*

****

Sade left Taylor's house and went to her salon to get her hair done by one of the other stylist. She was getting cute because Sylvia had set her up on a date that night. The guy's name was Tony.

Along with other illegal business Tony was the owner of Tip Top Cars, the car service that the girls used. He was having a private event at his home and he requested that Sade was his guest. She liked when she was requested by name, it made her feel like she was the hot shit it the streets. Sade had already gotten her outfit for the evening so after her hair appointment her intent was to go home and mentally prepare for her date. That all changed when Quincy called her.

The sound of Quincy's voice woke her girl up and made her throb for him. *Won't hurt to make a detour,* she thought before she went to his house.

Sade gave Taylor a hard time about Philip but she'd fallen for Quincy. The only difference was she was more in love with money than the thought of settling down.

****

Philip greeted Taylor with a kiss.

"You look beautiful baby."

"Thanks. I didn't know what we were doing or where we were going so I hope this is appropriate," Taylor said with a smile.

She choose a printed dress and scrappy sandals because she felt it was appropriate for anything Philip could have had in his mind; dinner, dancing, or fucking. Plus it hugged her body in all the right spots.

"Hell yes. You have my mouth watering over here."

"Good."

He smiled and asked, "Are you ready my beauty?"

"Let me grab my purse."

Taylor went toward the bedroom. She smiled when she turned around and caught Philip watching her ass.

"So no hint of where we're going or what we're going to do?" Taylor asked while they were in the car.

"Not at all nosey rosey, but I'm pretty sure you will enjoy it."

"I'm sure I will too."

Philip pulled up to the Hilton in downtown Atlanta.

He ain't wasting no time to get a taste of my cookie.

The valet opened Taylor's door and she got out. Philip quickly got out and grabbed her hand from the valet attendant.

Taylor and Philip went into the hotel and Philip led her to the elevator. To Taylor's surprise they did not get off the elevator to a room but went to the hotel's enclosed roof top restaurant.

They were led to a table that was next to a wall of windows. The view of Atlanta was amazing from the massive hotel.

"This view is beautiful Philip."

"Yes, but not as beautiful as you," he said as he placed his hand on hers.

His touch ignited a warmth inside of her. She made up in her mind that that night had to be the night Philip touched her from inside out. Taylor didn't know how much more she could take. Sade's statement slowly crept into her mind. *Damn, I hope he's not gay.*

Taylor and Philip had a good time at dinner. They never had a dull moment; the food was tasty and their conversation was outstanding. Taylor was grateful that she'd given him a chance and had not acted like a stuck up bitch.

They left the restaurant and got back onto the elevator. When the elevator stopped Taylor expected to be in the lobby, instead it stopped on the fifth floor. She looked at Philip crazy when he got off.

"Babe this isn't the lobby."

"I know but this is the way to our room."

Yes!

"Oh. Our room?" she asked as she strutted out of the elevator.

Philip grabbed her hand and led her to room five thirty-seven. He pulled out a key and opened the door. He closed the door behind Taylor and pressed her to the wall near the door. He grabbed her face with both hands and kissed her passionately.

"I wanted to do this all day," he said between breathes.

Taylor stood there with her eyes closed taking in every kiss. She felt his penis harden against her body. She wanted it. She needed to feel him in her pussy walls. She let out a moan at the thought of that.

Philip kissed Taylor on the forehead and whispered, "Can I have you tonight?"

"Yes," she replied drunk in his seduction.

Philip took Taylor's hand and guided her to the bed. He sat her on the bed and took a sandal off. He placed it on the floor and kissed Taylor from her toes up to her thigh before he removed the other shoe. Philip sent electric waves through her body as he repeated the motion on that leg as well.

Philip's kisses were so soft and sultry; Taylor's hormones were screaming. He lifted her dress over her head. Then he kissed her and undid her bra before he laid her back on the bed. Philip traced Taylor's body with kisses until he got to her panties. He used his teeth and hands to pull them off. He took a quick sniff and said "Ahhhh" before he threw them on the floor.

Philip had anticipated the day he would be able to taste Taylor. He spread her legs and kissed her pussy lips. Taylor let out a soft moan.

He handled her as you would a delicate flower until she had her first orgasm; at which time he aggressively used his tongue. He licked and sucked Taylor into a multiple orgasmic moment.

Philip took his clothes off as Taylor laid there shaking from the intensity. Taylor turned and looked at him as he opened a condom package. She'd seen him with his shirt off before and loved his six pack and tattoos, but she was surprised at his package; nine inches of thickness. The myth that white guys had small peckers went out the window.

Taylor could not wait to feel him inside of her. She moved to the center of the bed and waited for him to put the condom on. Philip did not disappoint her one bit. They made love several times that night.

****

"Why do you have to leave?" Quincy asked Sade after their smash session.

He didn't know what she did so she couldn't say she had a client to go see. Shit was getting real.

"I have to go meet Tay."

"You gonna leave all this to go hang with your girl?"

Damn, it is a lot too.

"Don't you have to go to the studio anyway?"

"Damn the studio."

"How about this? I go get up with Tay, you link up with your brother at the studio, and then we get together tonight?"

"Is that the only option?" he asked as he pushed Sade's hand between his legs.

Fuck. Be strong Shay.

"Yes."

"Okay," Quincy said defeated.

Sade gave him a quick peck on the cheek.

"I'll be back love."

Reluctantly Sade left Quincy. Money was waiting on her.

Sade did one last once over before the car picked her up. *Damn bitch you fine,* she thought as she looked at her reflection in the mirror. The black strapless jumpsuit and black and white pumps she wore was perfect for anything Tony could have in mind.

Sade's driver pulled up to Tony's lavish home. She'd seen some nice houses in Atlanta but his reminded her of Tony Montana's house in

"*Scarface*". She got out and walked to the massive door where she was greeted by a Hispanic woman.

"Good evening ma'am. Right this way."

Sade followed the woman into a sitting room.

"Mr. Lauratono will be right with you."

"Thank you," Sade said before the women exited the room.

Tony entered the sitting area.

"Good evening. You must be Shay. It's a pleasure to meet you. I've heard a lot about you," he said after kissing her hand.

"I hope it's all been good things," she said with a wink.

"Wouldn't you like to know? I like to do my own observation," he responded with a smile. "I hope you hadn't eaten yet because dinner is waiting. Follow me."

He placed his arm out for her to grab. Tony led Sade down a hall to a huge dining room. There were four couples seated around the table.

"Hello everyone. I would like to introduce the lovely Shay," Tony announced as they entered the room.

"Hello. Hi. Welcome," came from the group.

Sade put on her best smile, "Hello everyone."

Tony pulled a chair out for Sade and she sat down. She integrated herself into the party well. She held her own during the dinner conversation; she spoke elegantly and made sure she smiled a lot.

Dinner was over and Tony began showing his guest out.

"Shay come. Let's go to the pool."

"Okay."

Tony took her to a sitting area around the lit pool.

"So Shay, tell me about yourself."

"Not much to say. I love nice things and good company."

"So how long have you been working for Sylvia?"

"It's been a few years."

"A few years? So you've seen your share of men then?"

Shay didn't know how to answer that so she'd agreed, "Yes, I have."

"We actually have a common friend that I've heard you spend a lot of time with, Mr. Castello."

Sade became uneasy, suddenly realizing that her company wasn't really what Tony wanted that night.

"Mr. Castello?"

"Yes. Al Castello. Don't be cute like you don't know who I'm talking about because he's one of your regulars. So please don't insult my intelligence; especially after the evening we've had."

"Okay. I'm listening."

"Al owes me a lot of money. When he comes into town he always seems to link up with you and avoids me. I have a problem with that."

He moved his seat closer to Sade.

"When is his next visit Shay?"

"I-I don't know," Sade stumbled on her words.

"I believe you do Shay. Please don't make me regret the kindness I've shown you. I brought you to my home and around my close friends," Tony said sinisterly.

"He mentioned coming next week. I'm not sure when exactly though."

"Good girl," he said as he pondered his next move.

"This is what's going to happen. You will find out what day he'll be in Atlanta."

"But-" Sade attempted to interject.

Tony put his hand up to hush her.

"There's no but. You WILL find out. I do not know nor care how you get the information. You have two days. I will be in touch with you to get the information."

He placed his hand on hers.

"You're so beautiful. Please do not disappoint me."

He leaned in and kissed Sade gently on her lips, "Okay?"

"Okay," she said feeling uncomfortable. "I should be going. Thank you for a great evening."

"Alright, if you insist."

Tony walked Sade out to the waiting car and kissed her hand.

"Two days," he reiterated.

Sade forced a smile as she stepped into the car. She didn't know how much money Al owed Tony or what type of business they did but Tony's smugness left her with an uneasy feeling. She felt emptiness in the pit of her stomach. Sade did not scare easy but Tony frightened her. *Something is shady about that dude. Fuck! This is his car service so he knows where I live.* Sade tried to calm her nerves but she couldn't shake the creepy feeling she had. When she got home, she turned on her alarm system and called Quincy.

"Damn girl thought you forgot about me," Quincy said.

"Never. Come over."

"Okay ma. I'm on my way."

A calm swept over her.

****

Tony dialed out on his cell phone once Sade left.

"Hello."

"She just left. She didn't give me much, but I gave her two days until I call her. I'm sure she'll tell me when Al will be in town."

"Okay. I hope you're right.

"You know I'm not wrong often. I'll let you know what I find out about her and Al's business."

"Please because that little bitch thinks I'm dumb."

"You're far from that."

"Of course darling. I also need you to find out if her friend Taylor is involved in this side business as well. Good night," Sylvia said before hanging up the phone.

Chapter 9

Taylor was happier than a kid in a candy store. She was in love and everyone knew it.

"Ms. Jones do you need me to do anything for you?" Megan asked interrupting Taylor's day dream about Philip.

"Oh no. Thank you," she said still smiling from her thoughts.

Megan closed the door to Taylor's office.

"What's up Megan?" Taylor asked as she looked at Megan strangely.

"Ms. Jones I hope I'm not over stepping but I'm curious to what's up with you."

"What do you mean?" Taylor asked defensively.

"Not in a bad way. It's just that you're so bubbly and happy. I'm curious that's all."

"Curious or being nosey?"

"Well...nosey," Megan said with a giggle. "I know it's a man that got you all gitty. Your skin is even glowing."

"Really?"

"Yes, so spill it."

Megan took a seat and anxiously awaited the details of Taylor's affairs.

"You know this is so unprofessional right?"

Megan gave her an "I don't give a damn" look.

"I've been working closely beside you for four years now, one conversation will not mess up what we have going on. Hell, you listen to my men trouble all the time."

"Well...I've been seeing someone and I'm extremely happy. The end."

"That was watered down. I knew that much. What's his name? What's he do? Hell does he have a brother?"

Taylor laughed, "His name is Philip. He's sexy as hell and no he doesn't have a brother."

"Oh man. Wait Philip? That dude you met at Starbucks that time?"

"Yep."

"He was cute. I didn't know you liked white boys."

"Hell me either, but if I can help it I'm not letting him go."

"You better not the way he got you floating. I'm happy for you."

"Thank you Megan. Now get back to work."

Megan smiled and said, "Yes Ms. Jones."

Taylor couldn't help letting out a giggle once Megan left.

****

"Ma what's wrong with you?" Quincy asked Sade.

"Nothing."

"Your face says a hell of a lot more that nothing. Come here and tell me what's wrong," he said motioning for her to sit on his lap.

Sade sat down but didn't say anything until Quincy coaxed her into confiding in him. They'd practically become a couple without having the official conversation, so she felt comfortable enough to share.

"First off, I'm not just a hair stylist. I'm also an escort." Sade paused waiting for his response, but he didn't respond. "Did you hear what I said?"

"Yes. No disrespect but I'm not surprised about that. Once I told my brother I was feeling you, he told me that your girl was an escort. Hell, I'm not worried. I dick you down good enough that I'm sure you're not fucking on them dates. So continue to what's bothering you."

He was right about that; she wasn't fucking on her dates. Sade had even cut back on her Italian stallion.

"Well, I went on a date the other night with this guy named Tony. He was very concerned about one of my regulars. He said the guy owed him money and was dodging him. He asked me when he was coming back into town. I told him I didn't know but he didn't want to hear that. He told me to find out and he would contact me today. I did some research and supposedly Tony is the head of a crime mob; some Godfather type shit."

"Shit. That's heavy ma."

"Right. The worst part is he owns the car service I use so he knows where I live."

"Fuck bae! What you gonna do?"

"I ain't no snitch."

"Fuck that shit. You ain't got no loyalty to him. Do you?"

"We've been rocking for a while plus we've become business partners."

"Business partners?"

"Yeah. I've been working on the side. He's been hooking me up with contacts and he's gonna invest in me starting my own agency."

"Damn, sounds like you trying to make this shit a career."

"Uh yeah. It's good fucking money."

"Well that's a problem. How you gonna be my girl and still do this shit?"

"Your girl?"

"Yeah ma. Don't act like you ain't feeling this shit too."

"I don't know. I've never been the one to be booed up."

"Well it's time for a change. So be my girl and stop that escort shit. I'll make sure you straight outside of what you make at the salon."

Quincy kissed Sade and she forgot about her problems. The calm was brief because her cell phone rang.

"Fuck," she said when she looked at the phone; it was Tony.

"Tell him Shay. Let them motherfuckers deal with they shit. You don't have anything to do with that."

"Hello."

"Hey doll face. This is Tony. What's the word on Al?"

"He'll be here on Saturday. We're going to a banquet and afterwards he'll be staying at the Omni downtown."

"Good girl. You didn't tell him about our talk did you?"

"No."

"I hope not. If so I'd hate to spill the beans about your side pimping."

Sade gasped at Tony's statement.

"Until next time doll face."

Sade hung up the phone. Suddenly Quincy's request for her to chill with the business didn't seem that crazy. She did not want nor need Sylvia's crazy ass in her shit.

Chapter 10

"Good morning my love."

"Good morning," Taylor said smiling at Philip who was standing in a towel.

"Why you didn't wake me up? I could have washed your back, front, side, and everywhere in between."

"Damn. You looked so peaceful. I figured after the night we had you needed some rest."

"You were right about that, but know you can drop that towel and give me some more loving."

"Oh yeah?"

"Yeah," she said licking her lips.

"How can I resist such a lovely request?"

"You can't and better not want to," Taylor teased.

"You don't have to worry about that," he said as he dropped his towel.

****

Across town Sade was at Quincy's spot getting worked in his

shower.

"Oh Q," Sade screamed as Quincy had her pinned on the shower wall. He interlocked his hand in hers as he went deep inside of her. He kissed her muffling the sounds that she was making.

"Oh baby I'm about to cum," he said just before he pulled out of her. "Fuck," he exclaimed as he shot his cum into the flowing water. "Ma that shit's so good. Glad you mine."

Sade smiled as he planted a soft kiss onto her lips. Sade was content with her situation. For once the thought of being with one man was pleasing to her mind. Quincy was like a breath of fresh air in a room full of smoke.

Sade had been thinking about how she was going to get out of the escort business as clean as Quincy seemed to think she could. She worried that her decision to do business outside of Sylvia could bite her in the ass. *Taylor had always warned me about my hasty decisions. You really fucked up this time Shay,* she thought as she dried her body.

"So how did things go with Sylvia once you told her you were done with her shit?"

"Well...I didn't tell her."

"Fuck you mean you didn't tell her? So you and her expecting you to go on this date with that fucking Al dude?"

"Baby-"

"Cut that cute shit out. You not thinking this shit through Shay. You not hurting for no money so what is it?"

"I'm scared okay," she exclaimed. "Big bad Shay is scared for once. All the fucked up shit I did is coming around full circle. Sylvia all fly and cute and shit but she's a ruthless bitch. I've witnessed her fuck people up. My sneakiness and pride had me with the case of the big head but her and that motherfucking Tony are the truth! I've been trying to figure out how to get out this shit with all my limbs and more importantly my life."

"I hear you but first off know that I'm not going to let anything happen to you. This is what I think you should do. First cancel that date."

"But I-"

"Wait listen. Then you need to ease out by cutting your dates back to like one a week. No fucking though Shay. Don't get fucked up."

"Whatever Q."

"Do this for about a month and then tell Sylvia me and you getting serious and I want you to quit. As for the side business you may need to do two of the four dates for free; give her the loot. You can either tell her you fucked up briefly and that's to make it right or feed her some bullshit about respecting what she does and the money is a parting gift."

"That part's okay but I can't cancel the date for tonight. It's a pretty big event and Sylvia will have my hid."

"Okay have your girl do it for you."

"She ain't gonna do it. She's damn near, if not already quit."

"That's your best friend though. I know you got some favors in reserve."

Sade immediately thought about the favor she had from the Alfred gig.

"You're right. I'm going to stop by her house when I leave here."

Quincy was happy that Sade was finally seeing things from his prospective and smiled from ear to ear.

Damn, he so sexy. Make me want to- stay focused Shay. I got to think of a good story to tell Tay or she is not going to go for this. Hmmmmm.

****

"Baby you sure you don't want to come?"

"I'm sure. You go and have a good time with Billy. I think I've borrowed his uncle enough. You don't worry about me. I'll entertain myself; catch up on the things I've been neglecting since I've been in love."

Philip had a huge grin on his face.

"You're beautiful baby. I'm so glad you gave me a chance. Know I plan on keeping you happy. My goal is for you to be the happiest woman in the world. Now stop kissing on me before I don't leave here and I have my way with you around the whole house."

"Well damn. I don't know if I should be excited or nervous."

"I don't know either but I do know you'd be pleased; probably exhausted though."

"Alrighty then. Well, let's get you ready to get to Billy. Your fishing trip awaits you."

Philip laughed and said, "Seems like somebody's a little scared. Let me get out of here since you're being chicken."

"Whatever," Taylor said.

Truth be told she was a little afraid. She was still sore from their late night and early morning sessions. She planned to go to the spa and get pampered.

Her doorbell rang. *Saved by the bell. Who could it be though?*

Taylor went to the door. “Who is it?”

“Shay.”

Taylor opened the door.

“Hey girl. What you doing on this side of town?”

“Damn a girl can’t come to see her best friend?”

“Oh hell. What you need or what you done did?”

“I’m hurt Tay.”

Philip came out of the bedroom.

“Morning Shay. How’s it going?”

“Morning. Maintaining.”

“That’s good. Babe I’m about to go.”

“Okay honey be careful and have a good time.”

“Okay baby.” He leaned in, kissed her, and whispered in her ear, “Be ready for at least two rounds tonight.”

Taylor let out a giggle and Sade rolled her eyes.

“Y’all two! Glad I didn’t eat yet.”

“Good thing.”

“Y’all ladies have a good day,” Philip said before he left.

“Somebody’s all in love and shit.”

“Yes. He really makes me happy Shay.”

“That’s good.”

“So what’s up? Spill it.”

“I need a favor.”

"I'm listening."

"I need you to do a job for me tonight."

"Sade, I'm out the business. I'm done with that lifestyle."

"I hear you Tay but your accountant salary cannot allow you to do the things we do and have done; the money, clothes, shoes, and trips. How many people we know can say they've been chartered to private islands?"

"It's more to life than those things. It was fun, but now I want love. I want that happily ever after that I've been shitted out of so many times before."

"Damn, Philip must be laying some good pipe. But I get it. You've always been on that love type shit."

"Glad you understand. I hope you get on that soon. You're a great girl and you can't be doing this shit forever."

"Damn. You sound like Q. I will but until then I have this date set. Please do this very last job for me. Al is one of my regular sugar daddies. I need to keep him happy. If I could I would, but I have to go handle something for my mom. I need you. Plus you still owe me from that Alfred shit. Please."

Reluctantly Taylor said, "Okay Shay, but this is absolutely it. I mean it."

Sade gave Taylor a big hug. She filled her in on the details of the date. Sade ensured that she told Taylor to just go to the dinner party. She didn't worry about Taylor getting caught up in Al's bullshit because she didn't even want to go on the date let alone go back to the hotel with him. Sade was happy that Taylor never asked her what she had to do for her mother because she hadn't thought that far into her lie.

****

Though Taylor didn't want to go on the date, the dinner party turned out to be fun and informative. Taylor and Albert hit it off well. She found out that he was huge into investing and had an extensive portfolio as well as he was working on franchising a smoothie bar in Atlanta.

"I must admit Virtue that I was disappointed when Shay told me she couldn't make our date, but it has turned out to be a wonderful evening. You are an exquisite woman; beautiful and extremely intelligent."

"Thank you Al."

"No thank you. I'm serious about wanting to help you. If you have some time after this maybe you can come to my hotel."

Taylor tensed a little. Albert realized the situation in which they met and quickly added.

"No strings attached. I'd love to get to my computer and show you the things I've been telling you about. That's it. I promise."

"Well let me make a quick phone call and I'll you know."

"No problem."

"Excuse me."

She went to the bathroom and pulled her phone out. She saw that she'd missed a text from Philip.

"Baby, going to be in late haven't left the lake house yet. Hope you don't mind. Billy is having a ball. I love you."

She texted back "Okay" and "I love you."

Guess it won't hurt to swing by Al's. Thirty minutes tops.

Taylor checked her reflection in the mirror and went back to Albert.

"Okay it's a date."

"Cool. I'll be ready to leave in a minute. Let's do one more time around the room."

Taylor grabbed his arm and they mingled some more before leaving. Taylor drove so she met Albert at his hotel room. Not walking in with him may be the only thing that might get her out of the situation because Tony's goons, who were staked outside of hotel awaiting orders, thought Albert was alone.

Chapter 11

Albert was the perfect gentleman and kept his word; no strings attached. He'd given Taylor stock buy in tips and showed her ways to get into franchising with little to no risk.

"Thank you so much Al. I'm really going to have to get going."

"My pleasure. I love to talk to go getters like yourself."

Taylor smiled, "May I use the restroom first?"

"Yes, it's right through there in the bedroom."

Taylor had just finished washing her hands when she heard the commotion.

"Oh shit," she heard Albert exclaim.

"Yes oh shit Al. You look real good for a dead man. You've fucked up Al. Sit the fuck down and listen," she heard a gentleman say.

Taylor tipped toed to the bathroom light switch and clicked it off. She did not want her heels to make a sound on the ceramic tiles.

She climbed into the tub and carefully closed the shower curtain. She listened to the commotion coming from inside of the hotel suite.

"Tony is tired of you dodging him Al. You didn't even tell him you were coming into town. He got to hear it in the streets. Here you go around here renting bitches, going on trips, and wearing tailor suits and shit. Rumor has it that you're even in the pimp business now. Where's Tony's fucking money?" Taylor heard the man say followed by the sound of a fist hitting flesh. She'd laid out flat, attempting to make her body as small as possible.

"Fuck this shit! Vince I don't have no patience for this muthafucka. He ain't about to come up off Tony's money. Let me do this fool," came from an extremely angry guy in between the sound of a cocking gun.

"Calm the fuck down, Bobby. The boss gave me instructions on how to handle this matter. Timing is everything little brother, but you can be the one to do him in when the time comes."

Lord please don't let anyone come in here. Especially not trigger happy Bobby, she thought.

Albert was getting smacked around pretty bad from what Taylor could hear. She grabbed the twenty-two she had in her purse and prayed. *Lord I know that I've been slacking on our time together but please don't let me die. Lord please.* Taylor was zoned out until she heard Vince near the bathroom door.

"Bobby let me drain my main then we can get out of here."

Fuck, she thought holding onto the gun tight. Vince turned the doorknob to the bathroom and went to the toilet.

"Ah," he said as he released himself.

His phone rang and he quickly shook and answered it.

"Yeah boss we got him. Nah, the broad wasn't with him...No disrespect. I know Sylvia is your girl and all but she need to handle her own bitches. Just saying boss...Okay...We're on our way out now."

He hung up the phone and left out the bathroom.

Nasty bastard ain't even wash his hands. What does Sylvia have to do with this? What broad? Me or Shay? I need to get out of here so I can pay Ms. Sylvia a visit.

Taylor waited until the three of them left and quietly got out of the tub. Taylor was terrified; her heart was beating a million miles a minute. Taylor waited a minute to make sure the coast was clear before she opened the door. She walked through the bedroom into the living space of the suite. There were obvious signs of a struggle was all over the room. *Poor Albert but I'm glad he didn't rat me out. Maybe I should do something. But what?*

Taylor poked her head out of the hotel room. She heard the elevator door close. She moved down the hall towards the elevator. She pressed the button and caught the next one down. Once Taylor got to the lobby she decided to take a side exit versus going through the front. Though she had five inch heels on, that was one time she did not mind walking at all.

Taylor made her way around the building when she heard a gun go off. She turned toward the alley when she saw Vince and Bobby. She heard Bobby say "But he grabbed for my fucking gun." Taylor's phone rang and they turned her way. Luckily she was able to silence the phone and turn the corner before they saw her. "Let's get the fuck out of here," Vince said before they left.

Taylor waited until they were out of sight then went and checked on Albert. "Virtue," he said softly when he saw her. She began calling the police as he continued, "I'm glad you're safe."

"Where did you get shot?"

Albert moved his hand from his side and exposed the gunshot wound. Taylor talked to the dispatcher and gave him the details.

"Virtue, I'm probably not going to make it. Tell Shay that I love her and she needs to stop her side escorting because Sylvia knows. I don't want her to be next. Take this key, go back to my room, go to the closet, get my suitcase, and then take it home with you. Once you get it home unscrew the bottom where the wheels are; there's a secret compartment. You're a smart girl so I know you'll know what to do with the contents. Go now before the police get here."

Fuck Taylor, what the hell have you got yourself into? Now I know which broad Vince was talking about. Shay stays in some shit. I'm going to have to stop fucking with her until she get her shit together. For real.

Taylor moved quickly back to the hotel. She was dang near at a run by the time she got to the elevator. Taylor wanted to grab the bag and get as far from the hotel as possible. Her feet were hurting by the time she got off onto Albert's floor, but she did not slow down.

Taylor put the key into the door and reentered the mess of a room. She scooted to the bedroom and grabbed the suitcase from the closet. She pulled the handle out and rolled the suitcase out of the room.

There was an ambulance and police cars lined up outside of the hotel by the time Taylor got outside. She eased past the gathering crowd and rolled to her car where she let out a sigh of relief. She needed to confront Sylvia but she needed to know what Albert had stored in that hidden compartment first.

****

Sade was curled up with Quincy on his couch. They'd spent the entire day lounging around. *I could get used to this,* Sade thought as she laid there.

Her phone rang. She looked down and saw Taylor's name cross her screen. Sade didn't answer it; she figured Taylor was calling to gripe about the date. When Taylor immediately called right back Sade knew something was wrong.

"Hello."

"Shay! What the fuck?"

"Calm down Tay what's wrong? What happened?"

"You mean other than almost dying? Oh yeah by the way that's what fucking happened to Albert!"

"What? Where are you?"

"I'm home opening up a suitcase that Al told me to get out of his room while he was fucking dying!"

"I'm on my way."

"Where are you?"

"At Quincy's."

"Quincy's? Your ass is supposed to be in Beaufort. You know what Shay, don't bring your ass over here."

"Don't be like that Tay. Let me explain."

"Fuck your explanation. Al also told me to tell you he love your trifflin ass and Sylvia knows about your side escort, which I didn't know about by the way, so you need to get out. Good bye Shay. Don't come around me or call me until you got your shit together," Taylor said as she pushed the end button.

"Tay. Tay."

Tears flowed from Sade's eyes. She realized her greed had cost her her friend.

"Baby what's wrong? Talk to me," Quincy pleaded. Sade could not formulate any words to say.

****

Taylor was furious with Sade. *I can't believe she's in Atlanta! I'm so fucking done with her!*

Taylor unscrewed the final screw and tugged at the suitcase until the compartment fell off. In there lied three stacks of cash, a large brown clasp envelope, and a letter. Taylor began reading the letter out loud, "To whomever is reading this letter, if you are reading this then that means…" her voice trailed off. She put the letter down and opened the envelope. *Oh my god. You got to be fucking kidding me. This day continues to get more fucked up. I can't deal with this shit right now. I'm going to shower, wait for Philip, fuck his brains out, work on this ring, and live happily ever after as Mrs. Philip Barksdale.* Taylor went to her bedroom and placed the money, envelope, and letter in her safe. "Until we meet again," she said as she closed the door.

EP Publishing Presents
Virtually
Challenged
An Escort's Story
3
National Bestselling Author
J. Asmara

Prologue

Sylvia paced the floor of her bedroom cussing to herself. "Fucking idiots," she said softly thinking about Tony and his crew.

Sylvia and Tony had been business associates for over twenty years but he never realized that Sylvia had him on her puppet strings. On more than one occasion Sylvia had Tony do her dirty work. Feeding him information on Albert Castello and his love for Sade was no different.

Albert had Sylvia in a sling about some of her extracurricular activities, particularly with the head of the police commission; the very married Wilson Abrams. Sylvia's ongoing affair with Wilson was the reason she was so secure in her business and did not worry about law enforcement.

Albert found out about Sylvia and Wilson's affair when he'd set out to collect anything he could on Wilson for leverage on some of his illegal activities. Albert knew he hit the jackpot when he saw Sylvia creeping around. He hung in there with his pursuit until Sylvia and Wilson gave him what he needed in his arsenal; a picture of them partaking in their guilty fetish play.

Sylvia sicked Tony on Albert in hopes of retrieving the picture. She had a queasy feeling ever since Tony told her about the botched job his guys did on Albert. *That piece of shit. His life isn't worth my time but where the hell is the picture?*

"I need to talk to that bitch Shay. I bet he told her sneaky thieving ass where it is. That bitch is lucky she's still breathing anyway fucking with my money."

****

Taylor ran some water for a bubble bath to go with the wine she so desperately needed. She shook her head as she poured her wine. Taylor could not believe the day she had. She hoped the wine would help her relax.

When Taylor saw Philip off to his fishing trip she had no idea her day would end with mayhem. *I can't believe Shay's ass,* Taylor thought still pissed off at Sade for bringing her into her bullshit.

Sade knew Albert was into some shady shit and Tony was looking for him. However she omitted that information when she begged Taylor to go out with him.

Taylor replayed lying in the hotel's bathtub listening to Albert getting beat by Vince and Bobby. A tear dropped as she thought of Albert in the alley taking his last breath. She did not know him well but she felt bad for the guy; especially because he had a family. She wiped the tear and guzzled the wine in her glass.

Taylor refilled her wine glass, grabbed the bottle, placed it on the ledge of the tub, undressed and got into the tub. "Ahhhhh," she said enjoying the warm water on her body.

Taylor closed her eyes to further her relaxation attempt. Unfortunately all she could think of was the contents of Albert's suitcase and his warning to Sade. Though Taylor was angry enough with Sade to punch her in the face, she devised a plan to meet with Sylvia to right Sade's wrong. Mad or not she did not want Sade to get hurt or worst killed over her side tricks. Taylor exhaled and shook her head again as she thought of how idiotic Sade had been in her decision to work behind Sylvia's back.

Taylor washed and got out of the tub as she thought more about the envelope. In her safe sat a gold mine for an extortionist. She had compromising photos and documentation on the who's who of Atlanta; both legal and illegal. From the quick once over she made before she placed the envelope into the safe, it seemed to her like Albert had been working on his collection for a while.

Taylor smiled as she thought about the picture she saw of Sylvia. She was naked with a pink dog collar and leash around her neck. She was being "walked" by a man with leather pants with the penis area cut out. Taylor chuckled because she had not realized Sylvia was into kinky shit like that. Though Taylor didn't care on a personal level, she had a feeling that it may be good insurance on a business level.

Taylor finished the bottle of wine. She drifted off to sleep until Philip came home and showed her how much he'd missed her.

****

Sade got excited when she saw Taylor's name come across her phone. After the conversation the day before she thought she'd lost her best friend forever.

"Tay I'm so glad you-"

"Don't," Taylor interrupted. "I meant what I said yesterday. I'm not fucking with you until you get your shit straight. POINT. BLANK. PERIOD. I'm calling to tell you that I went to see Sylvia this morning. Your debt is paid with her. With that being said I hope you fly straight and get your shit together."

"Thank you Tay," Sade said relieved by what Taylor had said.

"Don't thank me. Get your shit together Shay."

"I will," Sade said before Taylor hung up.

Sade sat there feeling like her heart had been snatched from her body. Taylor had never been that cold to her. In their thirty years of friendship they'd never so much as had an argument.

Sade's chest tightened as she felt the beginning of a panic attack. Tears burned her eyes as she attempted to breathe. She picked up the phone and dialed the third musketeer. *Chyna please pick up,* Sade thought as the tears streamed down her face.

"Hello," Chyna said.

"Chyna," Sade said through tears.

"Shay? What the hell is going on?" Chyna asked frantically. Sade was never the one to cry. She did not even cry when her grandmother died so Chyna was afraid of what was going to come out of her mouth.

"I messed up Chyna," Sade cried out.

"Shay you're scaring me. Take a deep breath and tell me what's going on."

Sade took a deep breath and then several shallow breaths. Sade got to a point where her words could be understood.

"I think I lost Tay as a friend."

"What? No way!"

"For real. I really fucked up Chyna."

Sade paused, sniffled, and then continued, "I begged her to go on a date for me and I knew she didn't want to. She was just trying to do right by Philip and be happy. That's all."

"That's not that bad," Chyna interjected.

"I haven't got to the messed up part about it yet. The guy Al got into a deal with this gangster named Tony."

"A gangster?"

"Yeah some *Godfather* mob type dude named Tony."

"Damn," Chyna said.

"Yeah," Sade agreed. "Tony had some dirt on some foul shit I had going on behind Sylvia's back. He said if I didn't tell him when Al would be in town he'd out me to Sylvia...so I told him. Q was on my back about quitting the business and didn't want me to go on the date. I knew Taylor would say no so I lied and told her I had to do something for my mom."

"Oh shit. You know Tay don't like lies or liars," Chyna added.

"I know but I didn't know what else to do plus I didn't expect shit to go the way they did either."

"Alright continue."

"Well, Tay went back to Al's hotel room and some shit went down. She didn't tell me everything because she got pissed off when I told her I was in Atlanta and not in Beaufort at my mom's. All I know is

Al is dead. She told me to stay away from her until I get my shit together," Sade said sadly.

"Damn sis. I'm sorry. Just give her time and she'll calm down. While you're giving her space, get your shit together Shay. Stop all the street shit. We're getting too old for that. You have a good man on your team and you're an amazing stylist. Focus on those things and stop running after fast money boo."

Sade knew Chyna was right. Chyna and Taylor were the closest thing to family that Sade had and she needed them both in her life.

"You're right Chyna."

"I know," Chyna said with a chuckle.

"Whatever," Sade replied with a chuckle as well.

"Thanks for making me feel better."

"Anytime love."

"How are things in South Carolina?" Sade asked.

"It's good," Chyna said quickly.

"That's good. Well I'm about to go and get my game plan together."

"Good. Love you girl."

"Love you too," Sade said before she hung up.

****

Chyna had been sitting silent in a dark room with all the blinds and curtains closed for two hours before Sade called her. She was excited when she saw Sade's name come across her phone because she needed a pick me up.

Chyna lied when she said everything was good; everything was actually horrible. She had been a prisoner in her own home for slightly over a year. Her husband Brian was diagnosed with post traumatic stress disorder after he returned from his second tour in Afghanistan. During the first stages of him dealing with his illness Brian shut down. He alienated Chyna and their son Xavier. That went on for almost a year. However, Chyna never gave up on him and she supported him the best way she knew how. Unfortunately the depression took over him.

Nothing made Brian happy; to include the Army that he'd once worshiped. He decided not to reenlist, not realizing the connection to the military was what kept him grounded. After breaking ties with the military things went hay wire.

The once quiet man became a beast. Brian's rants and yelling sprees got so bad that Chyna sent Xavier to Beaufort with her mother. Brain had moments where he was consumed with rage and would have blackouts. Those moments usually involved him punching and kicking walls or throwing things.

Chyna stayed with Brian to keep from being a quitter. She did not want to give up on her marriage the way her parents did. It had become harder to maintain her sanity and many days she wanted an out, but she could not bring herself to leave. So she walked on egg shells as her heart continued to cry within.

Chapter 1

One year later…

Taylor stood in front of the full length mirror looking at her reflection. The soft pink mermaid style dress she wore was gorgeous; the Swarovski crystals that covered the bodice shined in the sunlight. Taylor was overly excited because she'd finally gotten her happily ever after. She began to reflect on her life as she looked at her reflection in the mirror. Taylor's journey was a rough one; the past year not being the exception, starting with Sade's shit.

Taylor held strong to her word after she and Sade hung up the phone that day; she had absolutely no dealings with her. Fortunately for Sade she got on the right track. She was excelling in her relationship, career, and understanding.

Her first step in the right direction was Quincy. Sade stopped fighting her feelings and finally let him in completely. For once she was truly happy. Quincy showed her nothing but respect and showered her with love.

Sade went back to her first love; hair. With the help of the near quarter of a million dollars she'd accumulated thanks to Taylor's investment tips and help from Quincy, Sade was able to open her own salon in downtown Atlanta.

Seeing things manifest in her life the way Taylor always told her they could, brought her a different understanding of life. For the first time in her life Sade had hope. She finally put the hurt and pain she felt being her mother's reminder of her rape to rest. The ugly selfish money hungry blinders she had on were stripped away.

Sade built up enough guts to go to Taylor's job in hopes of Taylor meeting with her and not spazzing out at her workplace. At first Taylor sat with her face balled up; holding on to her anger. Her anger was the only real reason she hadn't given into how much she missed Sade.

Taylor listened as Sade ran down the events of the months of their separation. Taylor's heart softened listening to the great things about her, Quincy, and the salon. It wasn't until Sade shared the best of the news that all bets were off.

"Quincy asked me to marry him."

Taylor shrieked and squealed at the news. "Oh my god Shay that's great," she said with a hug. "I'm so happy for you."

Sade started to cry because she was happy to be in her friend's embrace. Taylor asked question after question about the wedding plans.

Sade wiped her tears away and said, "That's not even the best part."

"What? It doesn't get any better than that."

"Trust me it does. I'm having a baby."

"What?" Taylor exclaimed as she danced around her office.

"I'm three months."

"Wow. This is so amazing, I'm so glad you got your shit together Shay. I missed you. I can't wait to spoil the shit out of my niece or nephew. And Guess what?"

"What?' Sade asked.

"I'm getting married too!"

They sat and talked for a while longer. Their conversation ended with Taylor telling her about Philip's romantic lake proposal.

Taylor was still engulfed in that blissful memory when Chyna and Sade walked into the room.

"Oh my goodness you're beautiful," Chyna said.

"You're so pretty Tay," Sade added.

"Thanks guys," Taylor said with a big smile on her face.

"Really Tay I can't believe how beautiful you are. That dress was made for you girl."

"Thanks Chyna," Taylor said with blushing cheeks. "Y'all look beautiful as well," she added looking at Chyna and Sade in their hot pink dresses.

Chyna's fitted sweetheart neckline strapless gown hugged her body putting out all kinds of sexiness while Sade's one shoulder goddess style dress showcased the beauty of her round belly. The three all had a glow about them. The moment was perfect.

There was a soft knock at the door.

"Come in," Taylor said.

Her Aunt Julia walked in. She smiled as she walked to Taylor.

"You are absolutely gorgeous baby girl," she said as they embraced. Julia turned towards Chyna and Sade and said, "All of you are beautiful. I'm so proud of the women y'all have grown into."

"Ahhh. Ms. Julia," Chyna said.

"Thank you Ms. Julia," Sade said.

Their moment was interrupted by another soft knock at the door.

"Come in," Taylor said again.

Her uncle Bryant came through the door.

"Wow, you are stunning honey," he said with a big grin on his face. He kissed Taylor on the forehead and asked her, "Are you ready to get married?"

"Yes," Taylor said as she grabbed Bryant's arm.

"Well let's go everybody," Bryant said.

They all moved out of the suite. They made their way to the garden of the bed and breakfast; the very one Will proposed to her at. She decided to set the beautiful plantation house as her venue to honor her past love while starting a life with her new love.

****

Sade smiled as she walked down the pink, white, and yellow flower petal aisle. Cameras flashed from every direction. She was so happy to have her friend back and be able to take part in her special day.

Sade continued to walk and smile at the guest down the aisle. She got half way and her eyes locked in on Sylvia. *What is she doing here,* Sade thought as she concentrated on keeping her face soft and pretty.

Sade took her place beside Chyna. She stood there with her mind racing about Sylvia's attendance. Especially since Taylor had never mentioned that she and Sylvia still communicated. Sade had not seen Sylvia since the last job she'd done for her. She hoped that Sylvia did not still hold even a smidgen of a grudge about her stealing from her.

Sade's thought were silenced when Taylor and Bryant made their way down the aisle. Sade's eyes locked onto Quincy's and a calm instantly came over her. She smiled because she knew she was good. Quincy lived to make sure that she was happy and secure.

****

Taylor kept Sylvia within arm's reach. She decided to not sever ties after their meeting about Sade's wrong doing. At that time Taylor ensured Sylvia that she had nothing to do with the situation. During the time she'd dealt with Sylvia, Taylor learned her ways and respected Sylvia as a woman about her money.

Sylvia was finally ready to get out of the business. She'd made several million dollars during her twenty plus years of being a misses and had a nice nest egg put up. While Taylor kept Sylvia close to keep an eye on her, Sylvia did the same. She remained close because she eventually wanted to present Taylor with a proposal for *Exquisite Evenings.*

It had been a year since Sylvia had seen Sade so she was quite surprised when she saw Sade with a belly. *Holy shit. Shay's ass is pregnant. I wonder if one of the Johns is the little bastard's daddy,* Sylvia thought as she watched Sade walk to her designated spot up front.

****

Chyna shed tears while Taylor and Philip exchanged their vows. Her tears came from two totally different places. First being her happiness for Taylor and the second being the reminder of her happiness on her wedding day; a happiness that was as faint as someone else's memory.

Things with Brian and Chyna were on a fast downward spiral. He did not attend the wedding with Chyna; instead he was at home drowning himself in alcohol. Chyna did not care though because she was glad to be in Atlanta with the two people who truly had her back. The three days she spent with Taylor and Sade reminded her of the many plans they'd made about living in Atlanta. For the first time since Brian was diagnosed with PTSD, Chyna considered leaving him and moving to Atlanta with her girls. It pained her to even have such a thought but she was reaching her wits end.

****

"This is the happiest day of my life," Taylor said to Philip.

"Mine too Mrs. Barksdale," Philip replied. "And I can't wait to show you how happy I am to have you as my wife on the beaches of Fiji."

"Hmmm. That sounds pretty interesting. I don't know if I can wait until the morning. We might need to find a late night ticket," Taylor said with a sexy glare.

"Don't play because we can skip out on the rest of this reception," Philip said pulling her close to him.

"We will do no such thing mister," Taylor said giving a sideways stare.

"Even if I do this?" he said as he grabbed her ass.

"Hmmm. Don't even try it," she said melting in his embrace.

"How about this?" he whispered as he kissed her neck and earlobe.

"Ahhh...Well maybe that," Taylor said smiling.

"Let's blow this joint babe."

"Noooo...we can't baby," she whined. "The reception will be over in an hour baby. So let's finish celebrating with our family and friends and then we can celebrate together."

The passionate kiss she gave him quickly had him agreeing with her. Philip's mother motioned from across the room for him to come to her.

"Go ahead honey. I'm going to sit here for a minute."

"Okay babe."

Taylor sat and scanned the room. Sade and Quincy were on the dance floor bodies entwined. *That's how her ass got knocked up right there,* she thought with a soft chuckle. Sylvia was by the door chatting up Philip's uncle. *Ah hell. Hope Uncle Robert don't be on her client list.*

Sade had questioned Taylor about her reason for inviting Sylvia. Taylor explained that Sylvia was a business connect that she never wanted to lose sight of because she was well connected. Selling ass kept her in contact with some big names in Atlanta; names that may show to be promising when Taylor opened the brokerage firm that she was working on. She still worked at Brown & Brown but planned to be gone shortly after returning from her honeymoon.

Taylor looked around the room for Chyna. She found her ducked off in a corner by herself looking sad. *I know something's going on with her. I wonder when she's going to tell us what's going on.* Taylor decided to give Chyna time to share her problem on her own but until then she was not going to stand by and watch her friend be unhappy. Taylor told the DJ to play *The Wobble.* It was time to bring back their party days. She, Chyna, and Sade danced the rest of the night.

Chapter 2

Sade was in her office eating lunch while she had a break between clients. The further along in her pregnancy she got the harder it had become for her to be on her feet, so she sat whenever possible.

Tap Tap.

"Come in," Sade said.

Her receptionist Veronica popped her head into the office.

"Shay you have a walk-in."

"Are any of the other girls available?"

"Shanelle is, but she says she only wants you to do her hair. I told her you were at lunch and she said she'd wait."

"Okay. Give me five minutes and I'll be out. Go ahead and put her in my chair."

"Alright," Veronica said as she slid her head back out of the door.

Sade quickly ate the last of the chicken and rice Quincy had made for her before she left out of the office. Sade looked down to fix her smock as she moved to her station. When she looked up Sylvia was sitting in her chair.

"Hello Shay."

"Hello Sylvia," Sade said slowly.

Sade was at her maximum of Sylvia. She went from not seeing her in over a year to seeing her twice in the course of a few weeks. *What the fuck?*

"Don't you look lovely? You have a serious pregnancy glow."

"Thank you," Sade said still speaking slowly. She didn't know what Sylvia's angle was but she wasn't going to feel comfortable until she knew what she was up to.

Sade's facial expression expressed her concern and Sylvia said, "Come Shay. No hard feelings. By gones are by gones."

Sylvia smiled but Sade didn't trust her one bit.

Sade grabbed a cape and put it around Sylvia.

"So what do you want done to your hair today?"

"I want a cut and color."

"Cut or trim?" Sade asked looking at Sylvia's beautiful shoulder length hair.

"Cut. I want a pixie cut and brown and blonde highlights," Sylvia said confidently.

"That's a drastic change."

"I'm in a drastic place in my life."

"Alright. Let's get you washed if you are sure."

Sade sent Sylvia to the wash center with her wash technician. She played scenarios out in her head to why Sylvia was there. Yes, she was one of the best stylist in Atlanta but she was not the only one. *That bitch is up to something. I know it.*

****

Chyna hated to go back to her reality after Taylor's wedding. It was the same old thing in her house; Brian's drunken fits, her on egg shells, and Xavier never wanting to be there. Chyna had gotten tired of her situation. "Damn I look bad," she said looking at her reflection in the bathroom mirror. She looked beat down; her once shiny hair was stringy and dull and she had bags under her eyes.

Chyna got dressed and went for a day of pampering; leaving Brian on the couch passed out. Chyna went to Elite Salon & Spa. She got her hair and makeup done, a massage, a facial, and a manicure. Afterwards Chyna decided she would go get a new outfit. She went to a shopping center called The Village at Sandhill versus the mall so she could enjoy some fresh air between stores. Plus there was an ice cream shop she'd planned on visiting.

Chyna was looking and feeling good as she moved about the shopping center. She'd just come out of Victoria's Secret when she heard someone call her. Chyna turned toward the voice.

"Tim?" she said with a shocked look on her face.

"Hey baby girl," Tim said with a big hug.

"Oh my goodness it's been so long," Chyna said.

"Yes, it has. You're still looking good I see."

"Thank you," she replied blushing.

"Where are you on your way to?" Tim asked.

"Marble Slab to get some ice cream."

"You mind if I join you?" he asked giving her a million dollar smile.

How can I turn down a man as fine as him? He's certainly grown from the blinged out wanna be seen guy. "Sure."

They engaged in some great conversation while they ate their ice cream. Tim filled her in on the years after the murder of his crew; Bam, Benny, and Mecco. He moved up north to New York after the execution of his boys. The streets had been talking and he knew he was next. He described it to Chyna as he made "a bitch move" and left. But he knew at the end of the day it saved his life.

Red, the guy responsible for the murders, had gotten picked up in connection of the murders. He was sentenced to forty one years. The members of his crew that were present for the beating of Benny all got fifteen years.

The reason Tim returned to South Carolina was because his mother fell ill. He wanted to spend the last year or so of her life with her.

Chyna enjoyed Tim's company. He asked questions about her and her life and genuinely cared about her response; something Brian had stopped doing a ways prior. The two laughed and talked for an hour. Before separating they exchanged phone numbers. Chyna felt really good about the day and refused to let Brian and his shenanigans ruin that feeling.

When she got home she kept to herself and avoided Brian. Chyna and Tim spent that night communicating via text. That was the beginning of many days and nights of the smiles that Tim put on her face.

****

Taylor came back from her Fiji honeymoon tanned, relaxed, and very happy. She walked into her office at Brown & Brown glowing. She was greeted by her assistant Megan.

"Good morning Ms. Jones. Oh I'm sorry Mrs. Barksdale," she said with a smile. "You look amazing. I wonder if the sun or Philip has you glowing like that."

"Well I'll never tell..." Taylor said playfully. "Has there been any major incidents while I've been gone?"

"Not particularly. Staff meeting is today at one o'clock. The updated balance sheets are in your inbox."

"Good." Taylor sat at her desk looking at the manila folder Megan neatly placed on her desk. "Thank you for keeping everything so organized while I was gone." Taylor and Megan had developed more of a friendship in the past year; especially when she and Sade were not speaking.

"You know I got your back. I just made fresh coffee so I'll grab you a cup."

"Thanks Megan."

While Megan was gone Taylor went into her bag and brought out a gift bag she had for her. She gave Megan the bag when she returned with Taylor's coffee. Megan quickly dug into the bag of souvenirs excitedly with a big smile on her face. She especially loved the "I got love from the Fiji Islands" zebra print shot glass.

"Thank you so much," Megan said.

"You're welcome. Now let's get to work."

Megan smiled and walked out of Taylor's office to her desk.

Taylor worked through lunch to make sure all her "t"s were crossed and "i"s were dotted for her staff meeting. She was walking toward the conference room when she ran into Alfred.

"Excuse me. Good afternoon Alfred," she said giving him her usual "fuck you in the ass" look.

"Afternoon to you Taylor," he responded dryly.

He walked off and Taylor let out a soft chuckle at the thought of Alfred allowing her to fuck him in the ass. She kept the footage in a secret file on her computer and watched it periodically.

Taylor made it to the conference room door when a gentleman caught her attention. It was Sylvia's boo; mister leather pants himself, Wilson Abrams. She wondered why he was there but didn't have time to investigate.

****

Sade fought the urge to mess up Sylvia's hair several times; especially with her sly comments. While Sade was coloring Sylvia's hair she'd asked Sade, "So I assume you are not still seeing Johns with the belly the size it is."

Sade took a deep breath and suppressed her crazy that begun to rise.

"That would be a correct assumption."

"So is the father that nice young man you met or is it one of your Johns'?"

Sade had had enough of Sylvia's slickness.

She spun the chair around, looked her in her eyes, and said, "Sylvia I've had just about enough of your shit. Either we're squared up or not but you will NOT come into my place of business with your bullshit. Who my child's father is or is not is none of your concern. I am no longer your puppet and you will not pull my strings."

Sylvia looked at Sade with a shocked look on her face.

"No one ever speaks to me like that."

"Maybe they should and you wouldn't act so crazy. So do you want me to finish your hair or do you want to leave?"

"Very well; I will not cross the boundaries of hair stylist and client anymore. Please finish my hair."

"Okay," Sade said as she spun Sylvia back around.

Sade got through her session with no more slyness from her. Sylvia loved her hair when it was done. She paid the one hundred fifty dollar tab as well as gave a fifty dollar tip.

"Thank you very much Shay. I love it," she said.

"You're welcome."

Sylvia was leaving when she turned back to Sade and said, "You really surprised me today Shay. I always looked at you as a weak little girl but now I see just how wrong I was. You have a good day."

Sade smiled as Sylvia left the salon. She felt a lot better about where they stood because it was evident that Sylvia was going to be around.

Chapter 3

Taylor walked into her townhouse that she and Philip shared until the closing of their new home took place. A sweet aroma of onions and bell peppers filled her nostrils. She was greeted by a vase filled with two dozen long stem roses as she made her way to the kitchen. Her cheekbones rose as she read the card. *"Thank you for making me the happiest man in the world. Love you always Philip."*

Taylor's euphoric feeling continued once she entered the kitchen to Philip in some boxers, a tank top, work boots, and a utility belt equipped with wooden spoons and a spatula. *Damn my baby's sexy,* she thought as she watched him working the pots on the stove; tattooed accented muscles bulging everywhere.

"Ah hmm...excuse me chef but I have a special request," Taylor said using a European accent.

Philip turned to her with a smile on his face.

"Anything for a beautiful woman."

"Ah...I would like a specialty dessert that will take some finesse."

"And what would that be my lady?" Philip said as he walked over to Taylor.

"I have the taste for some chocolate mousse."

"Chocolate mousse?" he said just inches from her face.

"Yes chef. A white chocolate and milk chocolate mousse that only you can give me. Right here and right now," Taylor said with a soft kiss to his lips.

The kiss turned passionate real fast and Taylor's skirt was quickly hiked up with Philip's hand in her panties. Philip sat Taylor on the counter and spread her legs. He placed his head at the entrance of her secret place as he spoke, "Before dessert can be served I have to taste your chocolate first. What do you think about that?"

"Sounds lovely," Taylor said regularly.

"Stay in character baby. Be my nasty foreigner."

"Very well, I will be Madame Elle," she said seductively.

Philip smiled before he dove face first into Taylor's hot and ready pussy.

"Oh baby," Taylor said as Philip devoured her.

Taylor grabbed Philip's head as her cum exploded in his mouth. The way his tongue flicked her clitoris drove Taylor crazy. She let out a squeal as she came again. She wanted to feel his thickness inside of her.

"Come. Fuck your nasty girl," she said completely engulfed in her developed character.

Philip got off of his knees and kissed Taylor as he dropped his boxers and his utility belt. Taylor got off the counter and turned around tooting her ass at Philip.

"Fuck me daddy!"

Philip obliged and thrusted all of himself inside of her.

"Yes," she yelled with ever forceful thrust.

Sizzles came from the stove from an overflowing pot but Philip did not stop. He grabbed Taylor's shoulders and went as deep as he could go. Taylor's body shook from the orgasmic sensation. Her pussy tightened around Philip as she pulled the cum from inside of him.

"Oh baby," he sang as he released himself of his seed.

They both stood panting as the pot on the stove yelled at them.

"Oh shit," Philip exclaimed as he ran over to the stove and turned it off. Taylor leaned on the counter in attempts to catch her breath. Philip moved her hair and kissed her on the back of her neck.

"I love you baby," he said.

"I love you too."

"Go get comfortable and I'll try to save dinner."

"Okay baby," she said as Philip gave her another kiss.

Taylor walked in their bedroom. On the bed was a robe and some Bath & Body Works' shower gel, lotion, and body spray. *Baby went all out today. Flowers, cooking, and smell goods. I wonder what the occasion is.* Taylor shrugged her shoulders and hopped in the shower.

****

"Damn," Chyna said as she laid in the bed after some amazing sex; something she hadn't had with Brian in a very long time. Sadly she didn't even feel the least bit guilty that it wasn't Brian.

"Damn ma that shit was good," Tim said as he laid beside her in the hotel bed.

"Yes it was," she agreed.

She and Tim had been communicating and seeing each other for months after their ice cream shop encounter. They'd kissed and petted one another before but that day Chyna was determined to let her itch be scratched by Tim. She had high expectation for him and he did not disappoint her.

She cuddled up to Tim and said, "Now what?"

"You mean other than us going another round?"

Chyna let out a soft laugh, "Yes."

"Well," he stated as he brushed a strand of hair from her face. "I'm going to wait patiently, with some coaxing of course, for you to leave your husband."

"Tim you know-"

"Yes, I know you don't believe in divorce, but we are good together. I know you believe in love and Chyna I've fallen in love with you."

Those words scattered her thoughts and she was too excited to think straight. She'd fallen in love with him as well. *What's a woman to do?*

Tim saved her from her thoughts and said, "You don't have to tell me how you feel because I can feel it. Just know that you deserve better and I'm waiting to give it to you."

"Thank you," Chyna said with a big smile. "So what was this about another round?"

****

"You have a collect call from the South Carolina Detention Center from Travis. If you would like to accept this call please push one. To block future calls from this inmate push five to decline this call-"

Rakeem cut the message off and pressed one.

"Yo Red," he said.

"What it do cuz?"

"Ain't shit. How you rocking it in the joint?"

"Shit. You know how I do."

"True."

"You get my letter?"

"Fosho."

"Good. So what's good?"

"Well mom's catering business is up and running. She's still cooking out the house now but she's looking to expand soon. Shit's going good for her."

"That's what's up. How's Big Mama? You found that humming bird for her yet?"

"She's good. I've been looking for it. I found this guy who knows a lot about humming birds; so I'll have it before her birthday."

"Cool. So-"

"You have two minutes left on your call."

"So stay up on that cause you know I'm not there to take care of things," Red continued after the operator finished.

"I got you cuz. I won't let you down. You be easy cuz."

"You too man. One."

"One."

Red gently bite his lip with a smirk after they hung up.

"What you all happy about Jenkins?" Lee's finest asked.

"You ain't got to know everything man. Just take me back to my cell."

The officer brushed off Red's slyness and walked him to his cell in Lee Correctional Institution. Red had spent five year of his sentence in the maximum security institution in Bishopville, South Carolina.

Red didn't have a problem with Officer Henderson but he couldn't tell him what had him smitten. It definitely wasn't any catering business or motherfucking bird. Rakeem and Red were talking in code. The catering business was in reference to his continuing drug business. Rakeem let him know that business was moving and an expansion was in progress.

Red had heard that Tim had returned to Columbia. He'd put Rakeem on the job of finding and killing Tim. Red didn't like leaving loose ends. He'd told Benny that he was going to take out his whole crew and Red was a man of his word. He felt good about Rakeem handling Tim for him. He laid across his bunk content with himself.

****

When Taylor got back into the kitchen after her shower Philip was making their plates.

"That smells delicious baby. What did you make?"

"Steak, rice, and green beans."

"Hmmm. What's the occasion?" Taylor asked as she helped him with the plates.

"Well..." he said building anticipation.

"What baby? Tell me!"

"Our silent partner came through! We are the owners of Barksdale Construction!"

"YAY!" Taylor yelled along with some hooting and dancing.

"Thank you for believing in me baby. I'm glad that you are not only my partner in life but also my partner in business. You're amazing baby."

Philip had shared his vision with Taylor many times while they were dating. She'd helped him created his business plan and as a wedding present she dipped into her investment money and invested in the business.

Though Taylor had mentioned her success in her investing to Philip she never divulged where the bulk of the money came from. She hoped she could go along in life never telling Philip of her life as an escort. The two ate dinner, watched a movie, and fell asleep intertwined.

Chapter 4

I*'m bored as shit,* Sade thought. It was a Monday and her salon was closed so she was at home. The apartment was so quiet that she could hear the refrigerator making ice from her bedroom.

Quincy had taken a more active role at Georgia Boy Productions with his brother Stacey. He was now the head of marketing at the label. With more pay came greater responsibility and more time away from home. Sade never complained because she knew he was doing it for her and their baby.

Sade's cell phone rang on the night stand near the bed. A wide smile came across her face when she looked at the phone.

She quickly answered it, "Hey Tay!"

"What up Shay?"

"The usual fat girl issues," Sade said with a chuckle.

"You're not fat just pregnant, so the bright side is you will only have those issues for another month or so. Can you believe you're about to be somebody's mama?"

"Hell no! But it's about to be so real in a minute."

"True. I can't wait to spoil him or her." Taylor paused, sighed, and continued, "Too bad I don't know if I'm having a niece or nephew."

"Oh boy. Here we go again. I told you I want to be surprised."

"I know but it's killing me to know Shay."

"Yeah. Yeah. So what's up?"

"You want to meet up for lunch and maybe some spa action afterwards?"

"Hell yeah! You're not working today?"

"Yeah, but I'm cutting out after lunch."

"Cool. Where you want to meet?"

"You tell me. You're the one with the pregnant belly," Taylor chuckled.

"How about that Thai joint near the spa?"

"Sounds good. I'll be there at twelve."

"Okay. See you then Tay."

Sade got out of her bed as quickly as her pregnant body allowed her after she and Taylor hung up. Sade was happy because not only was she not going to be stuck in the house alone all day, but she was going to do three of her favorite things, eating good food, hanging out with her best friend, and spa treatments.

"Oh yeah. Oh yeah," Sade sang as she looked for something to wear. "Oh," Sade said after a forceful kick from the baby. "Is mommy too loud? Sorry baby." Sade continued her preparation process with a soft hum.

****

Taylor couldn't wait to fill Sade in on all the new things that were happening in her life. Philip and his silent partner had been communicating constantly finalizing all the documents. Taylor had a meeting with the both of them at eleven that morning at Philip's office.

Taylor was also excited about purchasing her dream home; a mansion in a well to do neighborhood. The mansion was a foreclosed home from a former Atlanta Falcon football player. His misfortune was her and Philip's gain. Her real estate agent, Rayne Smith, got them the six thousand plus square foot home for half a million dollars; which was well under the one point two million dollar appraisal.

Taylor sat in her office with her chest out counting her blessings.

"Mrs. Barksdale, you have a call holding on line one," Megan said over the intercom jarring Taylor's thoughts.

"Thank you Megan," Taylor said before pushing the line one button. "Taylor speaking, can I help you?"

"Taylor darling. How are you?"

"Sylvia?"

"Yes. I hope I'm not disturbing you."

"No you're not but what do I owe the pleasure of this call and on my work phone?"

"Well, I have a business matter I would like to discuss with you and was trying to get on your schedule for lunch today."

Sylvia inviting me to lunch?

"I actually have lunch plans already."

"Very well. How about tomorrow?"

"Ah..." Taylor said as she flipped through her appointment book.

"Oh," she said remembering that she was to meet potential clients that week with the partners. "I'm booked up the rest of the week. Is it something that has to be discussed face to face or can we discuss it on the phone? If so I can call you on my way to my eleven o'clock appointment."

"I had preferred to have a face to face but the phone would be fine."

"Good. I will call you then."

"Very well. Until then," Sylvia said before they hung up.

Taylor sat there dazed for a little while after the call as she attempted to figure out what business Sylvia wanted to discuss. *If she wants me to go back to escorting she better think again.* Taylor continued to work on completing her task before leaving the office for the day.

****

Sylvia wanted to meet with Taylor after her meeting; a meeting that she should not have had any knowledge of, but she did. She wanted to present the opportunity of *Exquisite Evenings* to Taylor while her guard was down. *Slight change of plans but this may still work to my advantage. Give her something to think about after her meeting,* Sylvia thought.

"You know what you are supposed to do?" Sylvia said to her companion.

"Yes, make her feel cornered with no way out but to buy us out," he said.

"Don't get caught up in this shit darling. This is business.

Remember that."

"Strictly business," he said trying to convince himself. Taylor always did something for him. He still had not gotten over her. Their meeting was truly going to be a test of his strength. It had already been difficult working with Philip knowing he was with her every night. Shit was about to get real.

Chapter 5

"I love you Chyna. Tell me you love me," Tim said. Sensing Chyna's hesitation Tim went deeper inside of her vagina walls moving in a circular motion. Chyna let out a shrill of excitement. "Tell me. I know you do but I want to hear it," he added as he continued providing motivation. Tim grabbed Chyna's hands and put them over her head while he gave her slow grinds. When her eyes rolled toward the back of her head he instructed her again, "Tell me you love me."

Shit, I'll tell you whatever the fuck you want me to working my shit like this.

"I love you Tim."

"Do you really?" he asked as he sped up his tempo.

"Yes. Yes," she screamed.

"Good," he said smiling.

Damn it, Chyna thought. Admitting out loud made the feelings she fought hard to suppress, very real. The type of real that made her want to be with him all the time. The type of real that always brought her back to being married and miserable.

A whirlwind of thoughts quickly flood her mind as she looked up at Tim. *How did I allow this to happen? I can't love him…and be with Brian. I have to keep my family together. Well, what's left of a family.* Tim hit Chyna's spot and made her thoughts a faint memory.

"Oh Tim," she exclaimed as she showered him with her greatness. She had no clue what she was going to do about her little situation but she knew letting Tim go was not an option.

****

Taylor called Sylvia when she got in her car.

"Hello darling," Sylvia answered. "I'm so glad you could squeeze me in. What I wanted to discuss was my retirement.

What does that have to do with me? Taylor thought.

"Okay."

"Though I am still fabulous, I've been in the business for quite awhile and should move on."

"So how can I help you? Do you need an accountant?" Taylor rushed her along.

"Not exactly. I need you but not as an accountant. I've dedicated over half of my life to build *Exquisite Evenings,* which now is a lucrative million dollar a year business. Companion without commitment is appealing to people."

"Sylvia I am out of the escort business. I-"

"Yes, but you are a business woman. Taylor you are a very smart woman. You were smart enough to make the business work for you then and you can do the same now. I watched you very closely when you worked for me and I know you watched me too so I know you know the business. Please hear my proposal. You may find it to be beneficial."

"Alright Sylvia I'm all ears."

"Good." Taylor could hear her smile behind her words. "I know you have a meeting so I will get to the meat and potatoes. I want you to run *Exquisite Evenings.* I will give you all of my contacts, my books, as well as lend my services for the next year if/when something should come up."

Where's the catch? This shit sounds too good. Who gives away a million dollar company?

"All I ask in return is a piece of the pie for the next four years; forty percent the first year, thirty percent the second, and so on.

And there it goes. Not a bad arrangement though. Too bad I'm not in the escort business anymore.

"That is a very good offer but like I said I'm out of the escort business. I'm married now and moving on."

"I understand that but I know you Taylor. You like nice things and I'm sorry but your accountant salary cannot be satisfying your taste. I'm sure you're only making it the way you are because of the money you'd made while escorting. All I ask is for you to consider it and maybe meet me so that we can talk in person. How about I call you on Friday?"

Taylor had pulled in the parking lot of Philip's office by then.

"Goodbye Sylvia," Taylor said seeing a very familiar car in the parking lot. *There's no way,* she thought as she got out of her car and went into the building. Taylor's confusion turned to a mixture of anger and panic when she saw Philip sitting at the meeting table with none other than Alex; the crazy stalking psycho from her past.

Chapter 6

W*hat in the fuck is going on?* Red thought as he did his daily workout in his cell. He grew restless from waiting on a word from Rakeem. Red didn't want to make too many calls to Rakeem because he knew the phone calls were recorded. Red knew Rakeem would write him first, but the walls were closing in on him in his cell.

All Red could think about was getting vengeance for his brother. Red and Jerome were very close and it really messed him up when Will and his crew took him out. True he and Jerome were behind the two hits done to Will's stash, but in Red's mind it was no reason to kill his brother. The manner that Jerome was taken out also bothered him. *They fucking tied him up like a pig and then tossed his body for the motherfucking buzzards! Fuck bruh I miss you.* Red began punching the make shift punching bag he made with his mattress.

****

"You got to be shitting me," Sade said. Sade's mouth sat wide open as Taylor filled her in on her meeting with Philip and their silent partner. "That motherfucker's crazy Tay! I thought we heard the last from him and his trifling ass brother."

"Right."

"So not only did he stalk your ass but he waits all this time and HAPPENS to get into a business deal with your husband. What the fuck?"

"Girl, he sat there with this smug look on his face like everything was all good. I wanted to punch him in his shit!"

"Fuck yeah! You better than me because I would have," Sade interjected.

"I played it cool though because of Philip. I really want to keep the escorting part of my life a secret but that shit's coming full circle..." Taylor said as she sat back in the chair.

Sade did not like the sadness she saw in Taylor's eyes.

"What are you going to do Tay?"

"I have to protect my happiness. I WILL not let anything or nobody take my happily ever after away," Taylor said matter-a-factly.

Sade had seen that determination in Taylor's face before and knew she meant business.

"So what are you going to do?"

"I'm going to buy him out."

"That sounds good Tay, but let's be real he's a doctor not a construction man so it's safe to say he's made this move solely to get your attention."

"Hmmmm...You might be right Shay. I'm still going to try. If it does not work I may have to have a talk with Alfred."

"Good ol' sweet cheeks!"

They both laughed uncontrollably.

Taylor chose not to mention Sylvia's proposition. She intended to tell Sade but at that moment the Alex drama was enough. The two of them chatted about things such as Taylor's soon to be new house and their concerns about Chyna before their much needed spa session.

While Taylor laid on the massage table her thoughts ran on *Exquisite Evenings.* Sylvia was right. Taylor had an expensive lifestyle that was supported by her escort money; money that was quickly dwindling down. After the acceptance from the bank for the house cleared she would be left with just shy of two hundred thousand dollars. Taylor expected to allow that money to build interest to get her back to her million dollar start point. With the turn of events, Taylor had a feeling most, if not all of the money, would go to buying Alex out. The dollar signs of a million dollar escort service danced in her head. *What's a girl to do?*

****

Tim watched Chyna as she got dressed.

"So what would it take for you to leave him?"

"Tim, I told you from the beginning that I'm not leaving Brian. I took a vow until death do us part."

"Death do you part," he said stressing "death".

Chyna overlooked that and said, "Yes. So let's just continue to enjoy what we have going on here baby."

"Okay," he said dryly.

"I'm going to Atlanta this weekend. Tay is throwing a baby

shower for Shay. Do you want to go?"

"To a baby shower?"

"I meant to Atlanta period but you can come to the shower if you want to."

"Are you sure that's not going to interfere with your 'til death do you part vows?"

"Don't be like that. Brian doesn't go to anything with me and wouldn't know nor care if you do. So stop acting salty and come give me some love, cause you know you can't stay mad at me."

Chapter 7

Alex smiled at Taylor across the restaurant table. "I'm glad you called me...*Partner*."

"Don't be cute Alex. And you can wipe that cheesy grin off of your face."

"Feisty. I like that."

"Whatever Alex. My feelings for you have not changed. If it wasn't for you weaseling your way back into my life I would not be having this conversation with you now. With that being said, let's talk about this partnership."

"Ouch," Alex said as he took a sip of water.

"How much have you invested into my husband's building?"

Alex's insides cringed with her emphasis on husband.

"So it's like that huh?"

"Exactly like that," she responded sternly.

"You don't have to be like that Taylor. I thought we were better than that."

"I see you're still on this 'we are the world' bullshit so let me help you out. I'll give you one hundred thousand dollars to kick rocks."

"No."

"What do you mean no?"

"I mean the opposite of yes. It's obvious that you don't give a damn about anyone but yourself; not me or your husband. Especially, since you're interfering with his business arrangements. So with that being said, fuck you with a hard dick," he said as he rose from the table.

"How dare you-"

"No, how dare you! Have a good day partner," Alex said and walked off.

Taylor sat there pissed off for a minute before she regained her composer. "I'll get that ass," she said as she thought about her ace in the hole.

****

Alex sat in his car processing his and Taylor's meeting. He wished he didn't love her the way he did. She had a hold on him that had become too hard to shake. *Maybe this was a mistake. Why did I let Sylvia drag me into this?* The reason he got involved in Sylvia's plan was because of his loyalty. Alex felt that he was forever in debt to her because she'd saved his hide a time or two.

Sylvia made a malpractice suit disappear early in Alex's career. The judge that handled his case was a faithful customer of Sylvia's. She worked her magic and the case was ruled in his favor. As if that was not enough, his loyalty went even deeper than that. Two years prior she saved him when an incident went down with him and one of her escorts Brandi.

Brandi was one of Alex's regulars; the only female other than Taylor that he "kept". They did a lot of outings together and had lots of amazing sex. He and Brandi both enjoyed rough sex. That particular night he had gotten too rough and it resulted in her death. While choking her he applied too much pressure. He called Sylvia who in turn called Tony, who sent his men in to clean up the situation.

A few days later he saw a news broadcast that stated that an unidentified woman washed up on the bank of the Chattahoochee River. Alex was messed up for awhile afterwards. He had not been with a woman, escort or otherwise, until Taylor; hence why he did not want to let go.

Alex let out a sigh at the thought. "Damn you got yourself in a pickle," he said as he pulled out of the restaurant's parking lot.

Chapter 8

Rakeem grew impatient as he sat outside of Tim's house. He'd been there for hours and the empty food wrappers and soda bottles confirmed that. He huffed as he shifted his aching butt. "Fuck," he said as he tapped the steering wheel. "Where is this muthafucka?"

He grew angry as he fidgeted in the seat. As if the situation wasn't bad enough, his phone rang displaying "No ID". He immediately knew it was Red calling to check on his progress. He answered the call and pressed one when instructed to, excepting the charges of the collect call.

"Hey bruh. How's it going?" he said.

"You know...same shit a different day," Red responded.

"I feel you."

"What's up with the situation? You seen that fool since he got slick with your ol' lady?"

"I've been trying to see him, but he ain't trying to see me. He's been playing house with this chick, but it's always like I'm one step behind," Rakeem said shaking his head.

"Damn dawg. That's fucked up. You need to handle that shit for some closure. For real."

"Yeah I know. I'm working on it right now as a matter a fact."

"Cool fam. Well, I'm going to holla at you in a few days. I got some shit to handle up in here."

"Aight. One."

"One."

Red was a boss in prison so Rakeem assumed his "shit" involved somebody's face. Red's reach stretched wide. Family or not, Rakeem did not want to be on the wrong side of his shit. He decided to sit on Tim's house for a few more hours before he checked some other spots for him.

****

"Are you sure you don't want to go to the baby shower?" Chyna asked Tim.

"I'm sure babe. I'll chill here in the hotel until you get back. I don't want to be nowhere around when you explain me to your girls. You're on your own with that one."

"Whatever," she said with a smile. "Don't be scared."

"Shitting me. Your girls are savage."

Chyna laughed before she agreed with him, "Yeah, they are hell."

The truth was that she was nervous to tell Taylor and Sade about her affair. They'd never judged her but she always held the good girl title in the group. The conversation was going to be lit because she decided to leave Brian. She knew their reaction to that tidbit of information would be priceless. She decided to talk to them before all of the festivities started.

Chyna looked over at Tim who had just put their bags down in the hotel room. She licked her lips as she watched his muscles bulge in his linen top.

"Baby I think-" he started as he turned to Chyna. His sudden pause was caused by the fact that she began taking off her sundress exposing her matching bra and thong set. "Hmmm...that's what I'm talking about. Come show Daddy some love."

"Oh yes Daddy," she said happily as she pranced into his open arms.

****

Taylor had run around the entire day in preparation for the baby shower. It had been three weeks since her conversation with Alex and lots had happened. He agreed to allow her to buy him out for one hundred thousand dollars; with the persuasion of Alfred. After her and Alex's meeting, Taylor made a visit to his office. Their quick unpleasant conversation went like, "What do I owe the pleasure or should I say lack thereof for your visit to my office?"

"It definitely is not a pleasure visit sweet cheeks," she fired back. Alfred frowned but did not say anything to provoke another ass joke. "I need you to talk to your brother."

"About?" he asked as he sat back in his chair.

"Getting out of my fucking business. He conveniently got into a business deal with my husband and is being a dick about allowing me to buy him out. I need you to get him to change his mind."

"And how do you propose I do that? Alex is a grown man."

"I don't know nor care. Just make that shit happen or the partners will know about the dick in the booty moment we shared. Capish?"

"Yeah," he responded dryly with a bitch die look in his eyes.

"Good," she said pleased with herself.

The next day Alex contacted her about accepting her offer. She wished she was a fly on the wall for the conversation between the brothers and the thought made her smile.

In addition to the buyout she and Philip closed on their house. She was ecstatic and changed the location of the baby shower to her home. Taylor worked like a mad woman to get the house together. During that time she'd dodged several of Sylvia's calls. She was still on the fence about getting into bed with her, but she had developed a plan that she felt could work. Taylor had placed the final center piece on the rented tables when Sylvia called her again. *Fuck. Well I need a break so I might as well speak to her.*

"Hello," she said.

"Hello darling. I was starting to think you were dodging me."

"Dodging you? No way. I've just been extremely busy. What's going on?"

"Well, you know I'm about my business and do not like to leave any undone so I am calling about my proposal."

"Uhhhhh...honestly I'm not really sure."

"What are you not sure of? If you can do the job or not?"

"No, more so IF I want to do the job or not. Let's be honest, the money is good but the job isn't the most glamorous."

"Well, from my position it was glamorous. It is what you make of it darling. I see you've lost your fire and have gotten soft. It's okay, I understand."

"Don't bring that soft reverse psychology shit to me Sylvia," Taylor snapped.

"I'm just saying, you get some regular dick and you lost focus."

Sylvia hit a nerve and pissed Taylor off and she spat, "Don't refer to what me and my HUSBAND do, because you are doing the same with someone else's husband," before she knew it; admitting to knowing about her affair with the commissioner. *Fuck,* she thought.

"Ohhhhh...hmmmm...seems to me that someone has seen or been told about my extracurricular activities," Sylvia said acknowledging that she picked up on what Taylor had said. "Well seeing as you're so in the 'know' I'm sure you've seen that your dear sweet Philip isn't as sweet as you thought. Ha! You must not have Albert's black mail kit or you'd know that."

Taylor was shocked and said nothing.

"Oh so cat got your tongue? It's okay to put my shit out but not your darling husband. Grown up little girl."

"First, of all I'm all the way grown. Thank you very much. Second, stay out of mine and my husband's business. I don't care who you're fucking or not fucking, but just know there's no bitch in me. So don't bring your shit this way."

"It's about time you gain a boss attitude."

"What the fuck ever. You've pissed me off so check this; I will get with you tomorrow about this business proposition. You have a good day Sylvia."

"You as we-" she started as Taylor hung up.

What the fuck did she mean about me seeing Philip and him not being as sweet? It's time that I go through the entire envelope of documents.

Taylor looked at her watch which showed she had three hours until the baby shower was scheduled to start. *Good time,* she thought as she took the stairs two at a time to get to her safe that she placed in her office. She opened the safe and sat Indian style on the floor thoroughly going through the contents. Halfway through the stack of evidence of sex, lies, and thievery she saw a picture of Tony, Vince, Bobby, and a few other guys. Among them was Philip. He was a little younger then, but it was definitely him. *You got to be shitting me,* Taylor thought unable to process what she was looking at in the picture.

Chapter 9

"I'm such a fat ass," Sade huffed in front of her full length mirror.

"No, you are not. You're beautiful," Quincy said as he put his arm around her and rested it on her belly.

"You're just saying that because it's your fault that I'm fat."

"No. I'm saying that because I love you," he said as he spun her around. He met her lips with his soft full lips.

Sade closed her eyes and got lost in the kiss. "Hmmm..." she said once their connection was broken.

"You're sexy as hell to me Shay. Play around and we'll be late to this baby shower," Quincy said as he rubbed his hardened penis on her.

"Shiiiit. You ain't saying nothing but a word."

"What you saying then?" he teased.

"I'm saying bring that ass here and make me forget about being a fat ass."

Quincy bit his bottom lip and accepted the challenge. He gave Sade a much needed love making session. She'd received several calls from Taylor and Chyna, but did not care to answer any of them. Quincy always could get her out of her feelings and she loved him for that.

"Now I'm ready to go to the baby shower," Sade said with a big smile afterwards.

"Oh yeah? I think you concocted that hissy fit just to get some loving."

"You think so?" she asked in a sneaky tone. "You'll never know."

He laughed at her and they got dressed for their festivities.

****

"Say my name," Sylvia stated followed by a paddle swing.

"Oh..." Wilson said followed by, "Queen Sylvia." She forcefully swung the paddle again. "Oh...Yes. MY Queen Sylvia."

Sylvia smiled, happy about the scene she'd created with their new bondage chair. His ass was tooted in the air with his arms and legs bonded to it with straps. She'd dripped hot wax on him, whipped him, explored his hole with a vibrating bullet, and paddled him.

"Do I have your attention?"

"Yes."

"Yes whom?" she asked with another paddled swing.

"Oh...Yes My Queen Sylvia; my full attention."

"Very good. Now listen. I need Taylor Jones to be dealt with. I-"

"Dealt with?"

WAP

"Oh..."

"Do not dare interrupt me again." Wilson nodded his head and she continued, "I want her to be uncomfortable in every aspect of her life; starting with her job. Do you understand?"

"Yes my queen."

"Good boy. Do you want a treat now?"

"Yes my queen."

Sylvia gave a conniving grin before she undressed and force feed Wilson her pussy.

Chapter 10

"What's wrong Tay?" Chyna asked.

"Nothing's wrong. I'm good."

"Bullshit. You can tell the rest of these people here that, but I know you better than that."

Taylor tried to move past the picture she saw, but she couldn't. To make matters worse Philip had not made it home prior to the baby shower so she was not able to confront him.

"You're right. I'm sorry for trying to insult your intelligence with that. There's some heavy shit on my mind."

"I'm with you there. Let's get through this shower and then talk."

"Cool," Taylor agreed as they both watched Sade having a good time being measured with toilet paper during a game. Taylor was pleased that the co-ed baby shower was going well.

Philip came home near the end of the shower as Sade and Quincy were opening gifts. He said hello to the guest and greeted Taylor with a peck on the lips.

"I'm going to shower and then I'll be back down," he said before going up the stairs to their bedroom.

By the time Philip came back downstairs the majority of the guest had left and Quincy and the other men were cleaning up. Philip jumped in and helped. Taylor, Chyna, and Sade saw the remaining guest out and then went into Taylor's dressing room leaving the men to their business.

"I'm pooped," Sade said as she plopped on the chaise lounge. Taylor took a seat at the vanity and Chyna on an ottoman. "Thank you for doing this for me Tay. I love you so much," she continued.

"I love you too Shay."

"UH hum..." Chyna interjected.

"Thank you and I love you too Chyna," she added. "I'm just glad you came. You've been on some bullshit lately."

"I have not."

"I don't know Chyna. I think I'm with Shay on this one," Taylor chimed in with.

"So y'all double teaming me now?"

"Nah."

"No."

"Whatever," Chyna said with a hand wave.

"On the real Chyna, what's going on?" Sade asked.

Chyna took a deep breath, "I'm leaving Brian."

"What?"

"Why?"

"I'm leaving Brian is the what and because he beats my ass and

I'm not happy with him is my why," she said feeling free with the statement. She'd never told anyone to include Tim; though he suspected it. When she was bruised from a beating she stayed away from him.

"Oh honey..." Taylor said as she went and embraced her. "Damn. Are you alright?" she asked as Sade sat silent still in shock.

"I'm better than alright. I actually have something else to tell you guys."

"Oh hell," Sade blurted out. Taylor gave her a side eye. "What? This bitch just tells us that the 'love' of her life has been beating her ass and instead of telling us she's hurt, she says that she's 'better than alright'. Shitting me if this ain't about to be some bullshit."

Chyna rolled her eyes at Sade.

"Well...I've been seeing someone and-"

"...and the bullshit begins," Sade interjected.

"Shut up Shay and let me finish." Sade returned the eye roll to Chyna as she continued, "Anyways, like I was saying before I was rudely interrupted. I've been seeing someone and I'm extremely happy."

"That's good Chyna. Just be careful. Do you have a plan? Do you have money saved up? Do you need to stay here? Philip and I have plenty of space." Taylor questioned.

"No, I'm good. I have a plan. I'm telling Brian when I get back and I'm going to move in with Tim."

"Do you think you know this Tim well enough to move in with him?" Taylor asked.

"Hell no she don't! She thought she knew Brian's ass and

obviously she didn't," Sade spat.

"I do. He's not a stranger though. Plus I've been dealing with him for a few months now."

"Damn."

"Well I don't think it's a good idea but it seems like your mind is made up. I hope this Tim guy is a nice guy and is good to you. I'm happy if you are. Just know you always have a room here," Taylor said.

"Thanks Tay," Chyna said with a quick glare at Sade.

"Whatever bitch. You know I'm good if you're good. No matter how stupid that shit is."

"Whatever. Thanks. I know y'all would have my back. Tim was all scared to come with me to tell y'all cause he said y'all were savage," Chyna said with a laugh.

Taylor and Sade both looked at her crazy as she laughed.

"What have you told him about us to have him thinking we're savage?" Taylor asked immediately followed by Sade's "Damn this dude that important that you invited him to my baby shower."

"I didn't *tell* him anything. I told you he's not a stranger. Y'all know him and he knows y'all."

"Knows us?"

"How?"

"It's Tim; Will's friend."

"Get the fuck out of here," Sade said low key salty because they'd kicked it briefly.

"Wow. How'd that connection happen?" Taylor asked.

"I ran into him a few months ago. We exchanged numbers and

one thing led to another."

"Cool. Just be careful, because he's in the streets," Taylor stated.

"He was, but he's left the street life alone. After you know..."

"Yeah. Well as long as you're sure. Now onto my problem."

"Right. What's wrong Tay?" Chyna asked.

"Wait. Hold that thought. I got to pee. This baby is tearing up my bladder," Sade said jumping up as fast as her round belly would allow her to.

"Okay, I'm good now," she said as she waddled back into the dressing room when she was done.

"Okay. Well y'all know about the whole ordeal I was in when Albert got killed."

"Yeah."

"Yes."

"Well what I didn't tell you was that he told me the location of a shit load of black mail documents on the who's who of Atlanta; both on the right and wrong side of the law."

Chyna's hand went to her mouth with a gasp while Sade said, "Holy shit!"

"Yeah...well one of the pictures was of Sylvia and the police commissioner in a very compromising position. Shay you already know, but you don't Chyna. Sylvia has asked me to take over Esquire. I'm considering it; especially since I gave the majority of my saving to Alex to buy him out."

"Alex? Buy him out?" Chyna asked with a puzzled look on her

face.

"I'll fill you in on that later, but anyways. She's been hounding me about my decision and today I kind of let the cat out of the bag about having the photo. Her rebuttal was to nice nastily inform me of my husband's dirt within Albert's package."

"Philip?" Sade and Chyna said in unison.

"Yes. After we hung up the phone I went through the envelope thoroughly. Low and behold there was a picture of Philip in there; with Tony."

"Tony? Fuck!" Sade exclaimed.

"Right. It has me really messed up. I don't know what to do."

"Damn…" Sade continued as she reflected on how terrible Tony was and how happy she was to get out of his path.

"What do you mean what you're going to do? You're going to talk to your husband. Put that shit on the table and move on from there," Chyna said.

"It's not that easy Chyna."

"The hell it ain't. Let's not forget that your past is not squeaky clean. Stop being so dramatic. You love that man and he loves you. Fuck all that other bullshit. For real."

Taylor sat quiet for a minute and then said, "You're right. Thanks girl."

"You're welcome. Now let's get out of here so y'all can go check on your men and I can go to the hotel to check on mine."

"Hotel? So you brought him to Atlanta?"

"Yep," Chyna replied to Taylor with a smirk.

"Oh shit. Brian crazy ass is probably in a bush somewhere."

"Shut up Shay," Taylor said.

They all went back downstairs where the gentleman had finished cleaning and had returned her great room to its original state.

Chapter 11

Taylor was sitting in her office when Megan knocked on the door.

"Come in."

"Taylor Mr. Brown's secretary just called and said that he wants to see you in his office."

"Okay. Thank you Megan."

Taylor quickly ran down her to-do list in her head to ensure she had not forgotten anything. Arnold Brown rarely called her in; especially on a Monday. She could not think of anything that she had forgotten so she pushed the thought from her mind.

Taylor made her way to the elevator. She stepped inside and pushed "3". She hummed with the elevator music until it dinged and the doors opened. As she stepped out of the elevator Wilson stood there waiting to enter. He gave her a sly grin and head nod before he got on. Taylor didn't think much of it since she'd heard that the firm was a sponsor for a sponsorship banquet that the Police Commissioner Association was spearheading.

It wasn't until after her meeting with Mr. Brown that she realized that the visit was more personal than business related. That day she was told that her services were no longer needed at the firm.

Once she reached the office Mr. Brown and the other partners to include Alfred were in there. As the words were being said Alfred sat with a smug look on his face. Taylor wanted to slap the look off of his face but she decided to take the high road. She went back to her office and packed her things. Megan attempted to talk to her but she stopped her with, "I'll call you later."

Once Taylor got to her car she let out a defeated sigh. *I can't believe this shit. This is some bullshit for real. What am I going to do?* She replayed the conversation she and Philip had prior.

After everyone left from their home, Taylor called him into the kitchen.

"Hey Baby. What's up?" he asked.

"We need to talk. Like for real, for real talk. We hardly speak of our past and I think we need to now."

Philip took a seat with a confused look, "Why our past?"

"Because some things from our past have been surfacing in our present."

"Like what? I don-"

"Just bare with me. I'll let you know. But first I want you to know and remember that this is a no judgment zone between us okay?"

"Okay."

Taylor took a deep breath and said, "When we met I was into some shadiness." She paused as she watched Philip's eyebrow rise, "In addition to my accounting job, I moonlighted as an escort."

Philip pressed his lips together and nodded his head with a soft, "Hmmm."

"Sylvia that was at our wedding was our Madame, well Misses." Taylor looked at Philip expecting him to say something, but he never did. "Once we got serious I quit. Then the day you went on the fishing trip with your family Shay asked me to take a date; my last date."

"Shay?"

"Yes. We did it together."

"I should have known," Philip said softly.

"I owed her so I went. It ended up being a disaster. The guy ended up getting killed by a friend of your friend."

"My friend?"

"Yes Tony; the connection of our past. Before Al died he handed over his collection of blackmail evidence. You were in one of the pictures."

"Damn," he whispered before he explained his relationship with Tony.

"Tony is like family to me. I was a young jit in the streets being stupid and he took me under his wing. I started running numbers for him at first. Then I moved up to his collection team. I did good there so I was promoted to the 'muscle' gang. I'm not gonna lie, I've done tons of shit. Some shit went down in one leg of his organization and he told me that if everything worked out he wanted me to fly right because I was a smart one. Uncle T. hooked me up with a dude who owned his own construction business. Things worked out and I was out of the game. It's been a minute since I've hung with the crew but Uncle T. and I speak ever so often." Taylor nodded her head as she took it all in.

They continue filling in details on the events they were involved in closing their conversation with Sylvia's offer for her to take over *Exquisite Evenings*. They left the conversation open to a possibility. As Taylor sat in the car thinking about their new business with expenses, their dwindling bank account, new home, and her new unemployment she started to see the possibility as an avenue to look into.

****

"It's done sweetness."

Sylvia smiled at those words.

"Very good," she said to Wilson through the phone. "Mama has a special treat for you tonight."

"I like your special treats," Wilson said while smiling.

"I know you do. See you later."

"Later," he said before they hung up.

Sylvia leaned back in her chair and sipped from a glass of wine. "That bitch is going to come back to me now. My offer won't be as generous as before since she thinks she's so smart," she said with a sinister smile.

****

"Are you sure you're okay with this?" Taylor asked Philip after he blessed off on her taking over *Exquisite Evenings*.

"Yes. We really don't have a choice right now. We've put so much money into the house and business that if we don't do something we're going to be in a bad way. I'm looking into some things but for now go ahead and holler at Sylvia. Just for the record I still don't trust her ass, but I believe in you if you think that you can make this work. Be careful and know that it's only temporary."

"Alright honey. I'm on my way home now. I'll call her then. You hurry home because Madame Elle will be waiting on you."

"Hmmmm...I have a meeting with the architect in an hour, but you can best believe that I'll be home RIGHT after that."

"Good. I will see you later honey. I love you."

"Love you too," he said before they hung up the phone.

When she got home she called Sylvia who expressed that she changed her mind and her expected revenue would remain at forty percent over the four years versus the original decreasing amount. Taylor agreed to her terms since her intent was to not be in bed with her forever.

Chapter 12

Chyna and Tim stayed in Atlanta an extra day after the baby shower. Chyna enjoyed the additional quality time before facing her reality. She had anxiety the entire trip from Atlanta to Columbia regarding the conversation that she and Brian were going to have.

She'd told Tim about her intent to leave Brian and he was ecstatic. He'd even offered to go with her which was a big no-no in her mind. Tim did not want her to go alone, so after some back and forth they came to a final compromise. They settled on him waiting around the corner so he would be available to assist if there was a problem. Tim took her to her friend Asia's house, where she left her car, and then followed her home. He parked a few houses down while she went to her house.

Tim sat in his car with an uneasy feeling that he just could not shake. He stared at the house looking for anything out of the ordinary. His cell phone startled him as it vibrated on his lap.

"Hello," he quickly said seeing that it was Chyna.

"Hey Baby. I'm good. He's not here so I'm grabbing what I need real quick."

"Okay Baby. Be careful. I'll be right here."

"Okay," Chyna said before they hung up.

Tim breathed a little easier though he still could not shake the uneasy feeling in his gut.

Chyna rushed around the house and collected her things. She placed the final item into one of her two bags before she grabbed a piece of paper and a pen to write Brian a goodbye letter. When she was done, she called Tim to help her with her duffle bag and suitcase. He loaded her things, kissed her, and then they left for his house.

Chyna called Taylor on her way there. Taylor told Chyna about losing her job and her decision to take over the escort business before they got into Chyna's situation.

"So you really did it huh?" Taylor asked.

"Yes."

"Did he spazz?"

"He wasn't there so I left him a letter."

"Damn. A letter? That's fucked up."

"Yeah, I know. I'll have a conversation with him in a few days but I need space right now."

"I feel you. Just be careful sis."

"I am, so no worries. We just pulled up at Tim's. I'll call you later."

"Okay. Talk to you later."

"Love you Tay."

"Love you too."

Chyna parked and got out of her car as Tim pulled in behind her. She walked over to his car.

Tim pulled her into an embrace and asked, "Are you okay Baby?"

"I am now, these arms do something to me," she replied with a smile.

"Hmmmm. Is that right?"

"Yep, but those lips do even more," she said flirtatiously.

"Say no more," Tim said as he leaned in to give her a passionate kiss.

Their kiss was interrupted by, "How fucking sweet."

Tim and Chyna spun around to Rakeem with a gun pointed at them.

"What the fuck?" Tim said. "Take what you want little jit. We don't want any trouble."

"Trouble is what you got already you bitch ass muthafucka," Rakeem spat angrily.

Tim attempted to defuse the situation seeing as his piece was in his car.

"Look buddy I don't know why you're so upset but please calm down. Me and my lady just want to get through. Like I said, take whatever you want."

"What I want is for you to beg for mercy while you watch your bitch die."

Chyna let out a gasp after his comment.

"Chill mother-"

"No! You chill. You and your boys murdered my cuz."

"Your cousin?"

"Yeah Jerome. The other ones got theirs and now it's time for you to get yours. You're the last pig for the slaughter."

At that moment Tim's worst fear and his uneasy feeling both surfaced. He spent years attempting to escape his fate and it had finally come around full circle.

"Look..."

"Fuck all that. We've done too much talking already," Rakeem said with his lip turnt. "I'm going to do you girl first so that you can watch her take her last breath," he said as he squeezed the trigger.

Chyna let out a squeal as she got hit with the hot lead. Tim lost it when Chyna fell to the ground. Without thinking he lunged at Rakeem. He tackled him and they tussled on the ground until the gun went off. Rakeem got up still holding the gun and attempting to regain his focus from a head butt that Tim gave him.

He raised the gun to finish Tim off. As Rakeem stood there he briefly felt the barrel of a gun on the back of his head before it went off. His head exploded like a melon. Brian, who had followed Chyna and Tim after getting a glimpse of the two of them kissing when he was on his way home, ran to Chyna; who was bleeding out from her wound.

"Baby," he said to Chyna who was unconscious.

Sirens could be heard from a distance as Brian held her and wept. He paid Tim no mind as he moaned in pain from the shot he received in his thigh. The police made it to the scene and attempted to put the pieces together from the statements of Tim's neighbor who called 9-1-1, and two other neighbors with no help from Brian.

Chapter 13

Taylor sat with a fake smile planted on her face. She and Sylvia were having their first official business meeting. They both had resentment for one another but both were business as usual.

"So are you ready to speak to the girls?" Sylvia asked.

"Yes, I am," Taylor said as she stood up from her seat.

Sylvia led Taylor to the library where all of the ladies were. Taylor scanned the room. She saw some familiar faces as well as some new hires. Sylvia announced to the room that she would be stepping down and Taylor would be taking over; effective immediately. She watched as some looked enthused while others rolled their eyes.

"Hey ladies. I'm Taylor and as Sylvia stated, I will be taking over *Exquisite Evenings.* Though there will be minor changes here and there, things will primarily run the way they have been. I will be getting with each of you individually, but feel free to get with me if you feel the need to do so before I get with you. Until then it's business as usual," Taylor said before mingling with the ladies.

She was talking to a young lady named Camilla when her cell

phone rang. "Excuse me," Taylor said to Camilla.

"Hey Mama Toni," she said when she answered the phone for Chyna's mother.

"What's wrong?" she immediately asked when she heard Toni sniffle through the phone. She told Taylor about the shooting through tears. Her heart started to beat fast. "What? What happened? Is she okay? I'm about to call Shay and Philip and then I'll be on my way."

Taylor hung up the phone feeling like all the wind was knocked out of her.

"Sylvia I have an emergency. I have to leave. I'll call you," she said as she moved towards the door.

"Okay," was all Taylor allowed her to say before she bolted out of the room.

She ran to her car and called Shay.

"What?" Sade asked with disbelief.

"She got shot and is in critical condition."

"I can't believe this shit. Let me get my clients spread out to the girls and I'll be on my way to pack a bag."

"Are you sure you're up for this trip? My niece or nephew can come any day now."

"Fuck that if you think I'm not going with you," Sade spat.

"Okay. I have to call Philip. I'll be by your place after I pack a bag."

"Okay."

When Taylor called Philip his phone went to voicemail. She left him a quick message about Chyna being in the hospital and that she and

Shay were going to South Carolina. She had made it home and was packing her bag when Philip called her back.

"Hey baby. Sorry I missed your call. I left my phone in the truck. What's up?"

"I guess you didn't check your voicemail."

"Nah. I just called you back. Is everything alright?"

"No. Chyna got shot today."

"What!?!" Philip jumped in with.

"Yeah. It's crazy. She's in critical condition at the hospital. I'm packing now. Me and Shay are going down there."

"Okay. Are you going to be alright? Do you need me to drive you?"

"No Babe. I'll be alright. Plus you have those contracts to handle."

"Those contracts ain't shit if you need me."

A smile peaked through the distress and fear she wore on her face.

"Thanks baby. I'm going to be okay." *I hope,* she thought.

"Okay Baby. Drive safely. I love you Taylor."

"I love you too Philip."

Once they hung up Taylor finished her packing and went to Sade's.

****

Sade was packed and ready to go by the time Taylor got to her house. Her anxiety level was through the roof. Quincy was worried about her going but she insisted that he trust her to go, by telling him that she would worry more by not going.

Taylor sat and watched Quincy give a reluctant goodbye to Sade, "Don't overdo it Shay."

"I won't."

"I'm serious. Don't make me come down there. I need you and our peanut to be okay."

"I know baby. I'll take it easy. I promise," Sade said.

"Okay. I love you Shay."

"Love you too honey."

They shared a kiss before she and Taylor left. Unlike their normal road trips, the car was silent as they battled their minds.

Chapter 14

Whack-whack-whack came from the bathroom as Red landed the combination punch to the face of the inmate. Two of his goons stood on the sidelines and watched; shook by the whooping Red was giving the man over shorting him on his cigarettes. The whooping he got was about more than cigarettes though. He'd received word about Rakeem getting popped. That was family and it hurt. His hurt and pain then turned into anger when he found out Tim was still alive and inmate 2793679 got the bad end of the stick.

"Yo, the CO is coming," the lookout ran in the bathroom and said.

That didn't faze Red though. He was in "I don't give a fuck" mode and his cut off switch was broken, so Red commenced to beating his ass.

"Bruh, come on. Chill," his goon Snoop said as he grabbed Red's arm.

Red gave him a glare that pierced through him and said, "Get the fuck off me while I'm handling my business or you'll be next."

Snoop let him go and threw his hands up in surrender. Red stomped 2793679 who was a bloody mess on the ground by that time.

"Ah!" the officer yelled before he grabbed the radio. "We have a code red in the latrine. I repeat a code red in the latrine."

He instructed the others onto their knees facing the wall as he attempted to grab Red. His attempt was unsuccessful and the officer was pushed to the wall as Red continued in his violent rage. The extraction team came in at that moment. They laid high voltage of electricity into him with their tasers. Red finally stopped fighting and fell to the ground. They cuffed him and took him to lock up.

Red sat on the cement bench in such a numb state that he did not feel the effects of the fight or the tasers. After about an hour of sitting there "fuck" was all he could say as he shook his head. Tears fell from his eyes. He hadn't cried since he was a small boy.

****

Philip sipped on a beer in his man cave. He'd just spoken to Taylor who said that she and Sade had arrived in Columbia with no hiccups. He turned on the television and found the game, "Hell yeah. I thought I'd missed it. Kobe and them boys are doing their thing." His phone rang and he jumped to get it thinking it may have been Taylor again, but it wasn't.

"Hello."

"Hey Phil. How's it going?"

"Hey uncle T. It's going is all I can say right now."

"Everything alright?"

"Taylor's girl got shot today so shit's kind of fucked up right now."

"Fuck! It sounds like it is. I hope shit pans out."

"Yeah. Me too," Philip said as he took a sip of his beer. "So what's good?"

"Well, after we talked the other day I had my boys look into some things. As you know Sylvia has had Wilson in her pocket and bed for quite a long while. Like myself he's fallen victim of her grips to do her dirty work. As your wife suspected, Wilson did have a meeting with Arnold Brown. During this meeting he informed him that your wife had been tap dancing on the line of misconduct. He told him 'as a friend' that she came up in a drug and prostitute investigation that came through his division."

"That dirty bastard," Philip stated.

"Yes I agree. Don't worry about it. They will get theirs. I promise you that. Sylvia is a friend, but you are family."

"Thanks Uncle T."

"No problem. You continue to fly right and I'll take care of the gangster shit."

"Okay. Thanks again," Philip said with a chuckle.

"It's nothing. I'll let you know when everything is in the works. Ciao."

"Ciao."

Philip propped his feet up on the coffee table and relaxed feeling confident. When Tony said a situation was handled; it was handled.

Chapter 15

Taylor felt like there were weights on her feet as she walked down the hall of the hospital towards a waiting room. Chyna's mother greeted them as they entered the room.

"Hey ladies. She's still in surgery," Toni said through sniffles and puffy eyes. Taylor looked at her watch and realized it had been hours.

"Is everything going alright? It's been almost four hours."

"I know," Toni said in a defeated tone. "I wish they would say something."

Sade put her hand around her shoulders and said, "I know Mama Toni." Tears fell from her eyes. "Don't cry," Sade said as she embraced her.

Tears welded up in Taylor's eyes as she stood by. The surgeon came in at that moment.

"Mrs. Jamerson?"

"Yes," Toni replied.

"We are done with the procedure. It was successful. The bullet went through the left side of your daughter's liver which caused some hemorrhaging. It took us a little while to get that under control but luckily the bullet missed any large vessels."

"That's good," Taylor added.

"However she's in a critical state right now. She lost approximately a quarter of her liver. She will remain on close observation in our intensive care unit. I will not lie to you Mrs. Jamerson, the next forty-eight hours will be touch and go."

Toni let out a wail.

"When can we see her?" Taylor asked

"She's still sedated but you can see her now. Follow me."

Taylor guided Toni as she and Sade followed the doctor. Once they got to the room the doctor told them he had to do his rounds and left. Taylor's emotions were all over the place when she entered Chyna's room and saw her hooked up to all of the machines. Her eyes zoned in on the ventilator as the machine blew air into Chyna's airway. She quickly wiped a tear that fell from her eye.

Toni went to Chyna's side. She grabbed her hand and gazed into Chyna's eyes. Taylor watched and was saddened by the thought of what could have been on Toni's mind at that moment as she looked at her child.

"I'll be right back," Taylor said as she excused herself from the room. Her tears fell instantly. "Get it together Taylor," she said to herself. She called Philip who eased her mind briefly. He told her to stay as long as she needed and that he would take care of everything at home. They said their goodbyes and she returned into the room with Toni and Sade; who also wore the same defeated look on their faces.

****

"I need to see her!" Tim spat at the doctor as he pulled at his tubes.

"Mr. Simons you are not in any condition to go anywhere. Like I've told you, I will give you a report on Ms. Mack as soon as one is available."

"Fuck that! You've been telling me that for hours now. She has to be out of surgery by now," Tim continued as he tried to get up. His attempt failed due to the condition of his leg.

"Mr. Simons you have to remain still and stop pulling out your devices or I will have you restrained. I am trying to help you but I need you to comply. Do you understand?"

"What the fuck ever man. I need to know how my girl is doing. Point. Blank. Period."

"Trust me. I completely understand. If I were you and my wife was in your girlfriend's situation I would feel the exact same way, but as your doctor my number one concern is your recovery. Do not be fooled on the severity of your wound Mr. Simons. You are still feeling the effects of the pain medication. Just hours ago you had a hole in your thigh the size of a child's fist so you have to take it easy. You do not want to irritate the stapled area. So again I ask that you calm down and trust that I will keep you informed."

Tim let out a defeated sigh and said, "Okay."

"Good. Is there anything you'd like to make yourself a little more comfortable?"

"Outside of an update on my girl maybe some time without

people poking me every few minutes."

The doctor nodded his head and walked out of the room leaving Tim some alone time. His head spun as he replayed the events. It blew his mind that Red had come for him after so many years. He got caught slipping and Chyna paid for it.

Chapter 16

"So it's like that Sylvia? After all that we've been through?"

"Come on Alex. This is just business."

"Just business? Well our 'business' has never been done like this. I know what is happening here. You no longer need me so you're getting rid of me. You let everyone do your dirty work for you and then you dump them. I've seen you do it to others but I never thought you'd do it to me. I will have your money for you on tomorrow."

"Very good," Sylvia said smugly.

"Just know that the way you've been doing 'business' may bite you on the ass."

"Are you threatening me?" Sylvia asked as she sat up in her chair.

"Absolutely not. Just a friendly piece of advice my friend. I hope everything works in your favor."

"I'm sure it will. I will see you tomorrow then," Sylvia replied rushing Alex along.

He got the hint and walked out of her office. Sylvia expected Alex to pay her twenty thousand dollars for the business that she'd discounted him over the years. She told him that since she was getting out of the business, she needed to collect all moneys she could from "favors". Once he told her that was a ridiculous request, she reminded him of the biggest favor of all of covering up his murder.

Alex was pissed but made up in his mind paying her was worth it to get out of bed with her. Sylvia was burning bridges all across Atlanta with no care in the world.

Chapter 17

It had been five days since the shooting. Chyna had been touch and go the first two days as the doctor predicted. Her blood pressure had dropped tremendously and she coded twice. Taylor, Sade, and Toni had been a mess during that time but on day four Chyna came around and was on the better side of recovery. Though pained, she was awake and speaking. She was being moved from the intensive care unit that day into a regular room.

Taylor, Sade, and Tim, who had not left her side since he'd been released, were all in the room with her. They'd finally convinced Toni to leave and get some fresh air.

"I'm ready to go home," Chyna said in a soft weak voice to Tim.

"I know baby but you're body isn't ready for that yet," he responded as he grabbed her hand.

She had become antsy because Taylor and Sade told her that they were leaving the next day. They spoke softly to each other as Taylor and Sade were seated at a small table near the window.

"Are you okay?" Taylor asked Sade as she watched her shifting from discomfort.

"Yeah, I'm good. The baby is just moving a lot. The bigger I get the more it hurts."

"Okay," Taylor said not giving it any more thought, after all she did not make it that far in her pregnancy.

Sade moved to a recliner that was in the room and put her feet up in attempts of getting comfortable.

"So I was thinking," Taylor said to Chyna. "How about once you are better you take me up on my offer and move to Atlanta?"

"I don't know Tay," Chyna said.

"I'm just saying Chyna. What do you have here now? I mean besides yours and Tim's new found love anyways. Hell he can come too. I can have Philip fix the pool house up for you guys. That's one of the perks of having a construction worker for a husband," she added with a smirk. "Just think about it."

"Okay I will," Chyna said with a smile.

Their tender moment was interrupted with "Guys!" Everyone turned to Sade. "My water just broke!"

"Oh shit," Taylor exclaimed as she ran to Sade. "Hold on. Let me get a nurse. At least we're already in the hospital."

Taylor ran out and shortly after returned with a nurse who had a wheelchair. "Call Q," Sade said as she got hit with a contraction. Taylor nodded her head yes.

"He is going to kill us if he misses this," Taylor whispered to herself. "Chyna, I'll be back," she said as she went out of the room behind Sade.

****

Six hours later Zion Prince Hendricks made his appearance into the world. Quincy made it in time to be by Sade's side as she pushed. Taylor stood off to the side proudly witnessing the birth.

"He's so beautiful," Taylor said looking at the chunky nine pound baby. "Congratulations you guys," she added.

"Thanks," Sade and Quincy said.

"So much for going home tomorrow," Sade said with a chuckle.

"I know right."

"I'm going down to Chyna's room so I can show her the pictures. Man my nephew is so stinking cute!" Taylor said with a wide grin.

"Hopefully you'll get baby fever and have me a niece or nephew."

"Yeah he's cute but I'm about the money now."

Taylor handed the baby to Sade and left out of the room.

When Taylor walked into Chyna's room, she and her mother were involved in a conversation as Tim sat off to the side.

"Ma don't get me wrong, I'm very appreciative of him. It's just that I've been in my own personal hell for too long," Chyna stated.

"Hey everybody. How's it going?" Taylor said as she moved towards Chyna's bed. Everyone greeted her pleasantly. "What did I miss?" she asked.

"We were talking about Brian," Toni said.

"Yes. His mom came to see me. She gave us an update on him. He's in the VA hospital and finally getting the help he needs."

"That's good. So I'm guessing he's not getting charged."

"Right. It's been classified as self defense, but he did get charged with possession of an unregistered weapon and assault," Chyna said.

"Assault?"

"Yeah. He got charged with possession of a weapon since the gun was not registered. However, the assault came about because his PTSD kicked in and he spazzed on the officers. His mom bonded him out and checked him into the VA hospital for help."

"That's good," Taylor said sincerely.

"Yes, it is but I'm not going back to him because of it."

"And I don't think you should. Shit!" Taylor exclaimed before she remembered that Toni was there. "Oh, excuse me Mama Toni."

"It's okay baby," she replied to Taylor.

"So how are Shay and the baby?" Chyna asked.

"They are both fine. I brought pictures."

Taylor grabbed her phone out of her purse to pull up her photo gallery. When she did, her phone started to ring. She hit "decline" when she saw it was Alex. *What the fuck is he calling me for?* Taylor thought. Her voicemail alert went off as she got to baby Zion's pictures. She made a mental note to listen to the voicemail later. They all gushed with happiness as they looked at the newest addition to their family.

Chapter 18

"Oh Baby I missed you," Taylor said in Philip's embrace. She stayed in Columbia until Sade was able to be released from the hospital. Then she and Quincy convoyed back to Atlanta. Philip welcomed her home with roses, wine, and passionate love making.

"I missed you too," Philip replied as they engaged in pillow talk.

"So did anything exciting happen while I was gone?"

"No, not really. I told you that Uncle T. called right?"

"Yeah you told me about the bitch getting me fired. Back stabbing hoe!"

"Ahhhh...I like when you get feisty like that," Philip teased with a chuckle.

"For real though. So Alex called me the other day. I didn't answer so he left a message. I listened to it earlier and evidently Sylvia has betrayed him as well."

"Oh yeah?"

"Yep. He wants to meet about him purchasing Esquire."

"For real?"

"Yep. I'm thinking about taking the meeting because we don't want to be in this shit anyway."

"True. I say if we can have the money without the bullshit, let's do it. The buzz about the company is picking up so there's no doubt in my mind that business will be booming this time next year. Do you need me to be there with you?"

"Nah. I can handle Alex."

"Yeah, I know. Make sure you let him know that I'm not the average white boy and he'd get fucked up if he crosses the lines of business."

"I will baby."

Taylor had told Philip about their past relationship as well as about their last meeting. He was pissed at first because she spent the money to buy him out, when she should have come to him. He got over it though, seeing as he had secrets as well.

"I'll return his call later and see about meeting him tomorrow."

"Okay," Philip said rubbing Taylor's back.

"Oh that feels good Baby. It's been a crazy week."

"I know baby. Just relax and let daddy take care of you."

"I like the sound of that," Taylor whispered.

"Good," Philip said as he rubbed her body. "Let me take care of all your worries; mental and physical. I love you Taylor."

"I love you too baby."

Taylor fell into the safety of his hands.

****

"Bro why do you want to get into business with that bitch? You still sprung on the pussy like that?" Alfred said to Alex.

"No I'm not!" Alex replied. "This is strictly business; and maybe a personal 'fuck you' for Sylvia's bum ass."

"Yeah, I hear you. So what do you need from me?"

"I need for you to invest with me."

"Alex, I'm a partner at a law firm. I can't get caught up in this shit."

"And you won't. Trust me bro."

"Okay, little bro," Alfred said reluctantly. "I think you're crazy as hell to offer this broad four hundred thousand dollars, but I trust you."

"You're the best big bro. I'll let you know the details later. Now let's go so I can whoop your butt on the green," Alex said moving toward the door.

"Dude, you're delusional! You couldn't beat me if Tiger himself mentored you," Alfred said with a laugh.

"Okay. We'll see."

"Yes we will."

They laughed and made moves to go to the country club for golf. Alex gave no more thought to Taylor until their meeting the next day. One that proved beneficial to both of them.

Chapter 19

"Ms. Mack you are doing wonderful. You are an extremely strong woman. Your incision looks great," the doctor said as he pulled her gown back down. "As long as you continue in this positive direction you will be able to go home in a few days."

"Really Doc?" Chyna asked in an excited tone. "Don't get my hopes up for nothing."

"Yes really. If no issues arise you will be home on Friday. Three days okay?"

"Okay."

"Y'all have a good day," he said referring to Chyna and Tim.

The doctor walked out and Tim, who was still bandaged and healing, slowly moved to kiss her.

"I knew you were a fighter baby."

Chyna smiled the most genuine smile she had since the shooting. She and Tim handled the entire situation well considering that they both had a nagging feeling that blamed Tim; Tim more so than

Chyna. He had plotted revenge in his brain the entire hospital stay. As far as he was concerned Red had to die; no ifs, ands, or buts about it.

"Baby you hear me?" Chyna asked.

"Oh, no I'm sorry. What did you say baby?" he asked as he got out of his thoughts.

"What were you thinking about? You were zoned."

"Nothing. I think it might be these pain killers."

"Oh okay. What I said was, I think that we should consider Tay's offer. What do you think?"

"Hmmmm... It could be a good move. Honestly Chyna, I don't care where we're at as long as we're together. So it's your call."

Chyna smiled and said, "Atlanta it is then."

"Okay, but out of the hospital first," Tim reminded her.

"Of course," Chyna added still smiling.

Chapter 20

Sylvia walked into the rental home she and Wilson had for their sexual play. “I’m here darling,” she yelled from the door.

“I’m in the bedroom my love,” Wilson called back.

Sylvia walked in the bedroom to Wilson at the window.

“Hello darling. Why the face?” she asked as she kissed him on his lips.

“Oh nothing love.”

Sylvia looked at him strangely and said, “That is not a nothing face darling.”

“It’s a little silly, but I’ve been having an eerie feeling lately. As if I was being watched. I was just peeping out of the window to ease my mind.”

“Well, no one is watching us around here so can I help you put that thought out of your mind?”

“Please my love. Just remember I cannot stay long this evening. Tonight is Meredith’s benefit dinner.”

“Not a problem darling. Just know you will wear a smile tonight that Meredith will never put on your face. Come to mama."

Wilson's face lit up as he followed Sylvia to the bed. Once she undressed him his worries disappeared from his mind; a worry that was warranted because less than fifty feet from the bedroom, they were indeed being watched.

****

Officer Henderson completed his incident report. He was one of the two officers covering the lockdown unit where Red was being held. Henderson's report stated how he ran to Red's cell after several inmates yelled that something was wrong with Red. When Henderson got to Red's cell he was seizing.

He rushed to unlock the door as Red continuously hit his head on the cement floor. Once he made it into the cell he attempted to protect Red's head from further damage as his partner called the control room to call the paramedics.

In Henderson's report he went on to say how Red had stopped breathing by the time the Lieutenant on duty and the paramedics got to him. However, he made sure to leave out the fact that he'd slipped nitroglycerin into his food which caused him to seize in the first place or the fact that as he hovered him he covered his nose and mouth. Though tragic, no one was completely heartbroken behind the events since Red had been a pain in the ass since Rakeem's death. The proper reports were done and daily routines resumed.

Henderson's shift was complete. He dropped his report off to the administrative office before he left. He exhaled as he stepped out of the building and moved to his car; glad to be done with his twelve hour shift. He picked up his phone to make a call before he pulled out of the parking lot.

"Hey bruh," he said.

"What's good?"

"Everything is everything. He took his last breath today."

"Bet. Good looking out man."

"No problem fam. Make sure you hit me up once you and your girl get settled in ATL."

"Of course. One," Tim said before he and Officer Henderson hung up.

Tim smiled when the phone went silent. He'd had his man watching Red every since he'd transferred to Lee. Red had appeared to had been cooling so Tim had hoped the beef was dead. His complacency caused Chyna to almost lose her life and that was unacceptable. Though they say revenge is bitter sweet, there was only sweetness to Tim. He was able to avenge his crew's deaths as well as honor his woman. It was a win-win in his book with his and Chyna's move to Atlanta being a week away; a move that they both were ready to make.

Chapter 21

Six months later…

The three musketeers were together again. Taylor, Sade, and Chyna were all seated at Taylor's dining room table with baby Zion near in his play pen.

"I can't believe I'm getting married," Sade said as she looked at the table filled with wedding favors.

"I know right," Chyna said with a chuckle.

"Right," Taylor added with a laugh.

"Ha ha! Fuck both of y'all." The two of them laughed as she continued, "With a hard dick."

"Fine with me, cause I like hard dicks," Chyna said still laughing.

"Y'all are stupid," Taylor said in between her laugh. "But for real, I'm so happy for you Shay. Hell, for all of us because it's been a crazy ass six months."

"Hell yeah! But we all made it!" Sade said.

"I know I'm grateful because I could have died, but look at me. I'm still not one hundred percent, but hell I'll take ninety to ninety-five percent," Chyna said.

"For real!" Sade agreed.

"Then Tay allowing me to come here has been great for me, Tim, and Xavier. Having my son back with me is awesome in itself. Then as if you and Philip hadn't done enough, he hired Tim! Amazing!" Chyna added getting emotional.

"Don't you have all of us in here crying and shit," Sade said. "You know my hormones are still fucked up since Zi and you know Tay is all hormonal. But I feel you though. I never would have thought I'd be getting married this weekend, the salon is growing clientele like crazy, and I can't even express the joy I've found in motherhood. Y'all know I ain't never thought I'd be noooobody's mama!" They all laughed. "But I can't see my life any different now," she finished with a wide grin.

"Well, I guess it's my turn in our mushy show and tell moment," Taylor said. "I'm finally done with Sylvia and the escort life. Good fucking riddance to that."

"Hell yeah!" Sade cosigned.

"Ain't it! I can't stand Alex's bitch ass, but he came through and helped me replenish my savings. The best part of the whole thing was seeing Sylvia's face when she found out that Alex bought me out. That shit was priceless!" Taylor broke out in laughter, "That hoe was so mad!"

"I bet!"

"I know she was!"

"Alex and I did that shit so smooth too. I feed him all the information she feed me and waited until she got comfortable with the situation. She thought I'd put her sneaky tactics to rest, but absolutely not. She tried to contest the buyout, but we spent the past months putting our ducks in a row. Oh well, that shit's their problem now. I got my husband and our growing family to worry about now," Taylor said looking down at her little three month baby bump.

The ladies sat in silence as they all reflected on the paths their lives had traveled. Their silence was broken by Philip and Tim coming into the dining room.

"Hey ladies. Looks like y'all are busy here. Or are y'all faking?" Philip asked.

"You know they be faking," Tim added.

"There you go," Chyna said with a side eye.

"Get off my boy now. Y'all know y'all be doing more talking than working," Philip said as he walked over to Taylor and kissed her. "Hey baby. Can I talk to you upstairs?"

"Sure. Hey y'all I'll be right back. Make sure y'all working on the favors for real," Taylor said as she followed Philip. "Hell put Tim's ass to work too," she added from the stairs.

"Shiiiiittt. I just came from work," he said.

"You probably ain't even done anything," Taylor heard Sade say before she made it all the way up the stairs.

"What's up baby," Taylor asked once they reached their bedroom.

"Had you heard about Sylvia?"

"No, what are you talking about."

"Her and her love were killed today."

"Wow! What happened."

"Well, apparently the guy's wife caught them in the middle of their play session and shot them both."

"Damn. That's fucked up. They say what's done in the dark will come to the light."

"Yes it will. Especially when you have Uncle T. in your corner," Philip said with a smirk.

Taylor stopped, "Wait. What did you do?"

"I didn't do anything. Except maybe possibly got some information to Mrs. Meredith Abrams about her husband's long standing affair. It didn't play out exactly how I thought, but shit happens."

Shocked at what he said Taylor responded with, "You sneaky dog! I've never seen this side of you, but I must say that it's sexy."

"Oh yeah?"

"Yeah. If I didn't have all the wedding things to help with I'd throw myself across this bed for a quickie," she said in a sneaky tone.

"You know I'm down," Philip said pulling at Taylor.

Taylor giggled like a school girl, "I have to get back, but know that was some real shit you did for our family. I love you baby 'til death."

"I love you too baby. I told you that I got you. I meant it then but definitely now that you're carrying our child. Nothing nor no one will ever harm you as long as I have breath in my body."

Taylor smiled and they shared a passionate kiss before she went back downstairs. They left the conversation there and never mentioned it again.

Taylor went back to the dining room where Sade and Chyna had made head way with the items for the favor boxes.

"About time you came back. Shay has been a bridezilla over here," Chyna stated to Taylor.

"Whatever," Sade said as she rolled her eyes.

"Play nice ladies," Taylor said.

"There you go always being the peace maker," Sade said.

"Right. Every since we were little," Chyna chimed in with.

"Oh well. Deal with it," Taylor said with a chuckle. At that moment Taylor realized that they each played their own role in their friendship and they were not complete without each other. "I love you guys," she added.

"We love you too."

"Love you too Tay."

That Saturday Sade and Quincy got married in Taylor's massive backyard amongst family and friends. The musketeers embarked on their happily ever after; closing the door to the past. Chyna divorced Brian and was madly in love. Taylor was rich, free, and happy. That fall she gave birth to London Hope Barksdale. She moved forward never giving any thought to escorting. The only tie that remained of that life was the envelope that sat in her safe as insurance.

THE END

About the Author

J. Asmara is a national bestselling author of several works of romance, erotica, drama and suspense. The Beaufort, South Carolina native grew up as a small town girl destined for great things. As with most people, her life was not always fair, however she endured and overcame adversity. Her passion for writing evolved in March 2014 with her debut novella When It Raynes and she has no plan of stopping.

Website: www.authorjasmara.com
Facebook: www.facebook.com/AuthorJAsmara
Twitter: www.twitter.com/AuthorJAsmara
Instagram: www.instagram.com/authorjasmara
Email Address: theasmara@yahoo.com

www.ingramcontent.com/pod-product-compliance
Lightning Source LLC
Chambersburg PA
CBHW061519020726
47502CB00006B/2136

* 9 7 8 0 6 9 2 7 9 4 9 5 1 *